THE NIGHT RISING

RITE WORLD: NIGHT WOLVES
BOOK 4

JULIANA HAYGERT

COPYRIGHT

AUTHOR'S NOTE

I hope you enjoy reading *The Night Rising*!

Don't forget to sign up for my Newsletter to find out about new releases, cover reveals, giveaways, and more!

If you want to see exclusive teasers, help me decide on covers, read excerpts, talk about books, etc, join my reader group on Facebook: Juliana's Club!

RITE WORLD

Welcome to the RITE WORLD!

Free Novellas:
The Vampire Hunt
The Light Witch

Novellas:
The Hunter Path
The Light Calling
The Light Witch
The Wicked Alliance
The Shadow Fae

Rite World:
The Vampire Heir (Book 1)
The Witch Queen (Book 2)
The Immortal Vow (Book 3)

The Warlock Lord (Book 4)
The Wolf Consort (Book 5)
The Crystal Rose (Book 6)
The Wolf Forsaken (Book 7)
The Fae Bound (Book 8)
The Blood Pact (Book 9)

Rite World: Blackthorn Hunters Academy
The Demons Kiss (Book 1)
The Hunter Secret (Book 2)
The Soul Bond (Book 3)
The Shadow Trials (Book 4)
The Immortal Vow (Book 5)

Rite World: Vampire Wars
The Darkest Vampire (Book 1)
The Darkest Witch (Book 2)
The Darkest Magic (Book 3)

Rite World: Night Wolves
The Night Calling (Book 1)
The Night Burning (Book 2)
The Night Hunting (Book 3)
The Night Rising (Book 4)

Rite World: Lightgrove Witches
The Midnight Test (Book 1)
The Midnight Spell (Book 2)
The Midnight Flame (Book 3)

And more to come!

1

SHANE

Fire covered Raika's body, the flames high and strong like a bonfire.

For half a second, I watched in shock. Then I acted. "Raika?" my trembling voice called. Fear gripped my insides as I tried reaching for her. The fire flickered, sending embers my way, and the heat singed the hairs from my arms. I flinched, my despair growing.

I grabbed my phone and—

The fire died.

Just like that. One second, it felt like it would explode and spread across the entire village, the next it was gone.

Raika stood there, her eyes half-closed, her lips parted, her skin covered in soot. Her clothes were in tatters, but she wasn't burned.

"Raika?" I took a step closer to her. The heat was still there, but not nearly as bad as before.

Raika let out a long sigh and fell back.

I dashed to her and caught her before she hit the ground.

Her hot body burned my skin, and I hissed. Cradling her in my arms, I ran to the infirmary.

Jay's face paled as he saw us coming. "What—?"

"Help me," I asked, my voice frantic.

"I ..." He was in shock. "I don't have supplies yet. It's better if—"

I didn't hear him finish. I ran to DuMoir Castle.

I yelled as I approached one of the guarded side doors. "Help!" The two vampire guards stood at attention. "I need a healer! Now!"

One of them disappeared inside the castle, while the other came to me. "What happened?" He glanced behind us, as if looking for an imminent threat. "Who did this?"

"No one," I whispered, still stunned with what had happened. "It was her."

The guard balked at me and halted. I ran into the castle, toward the infirmary. Rapid footsteps sounded through the corridors. Prince Killian and Lavinia faltered as they took in Raika in my arms.

"What happened?" Killian asked.

"I ..." I shook my head and kept going. They followed me.

The infirmary was located in the east wing of the castle, on the first floor. It was a large room with a handful of hospital beds, and a couple of doors in the back led to private rooms.

I laid Raika on one of the beds as a female vampire stepped closer. "What happened?" she asked. I growled at her, not willing to let anyone touch my mate. The female shot me a stern look. "If you want me to help her, back off." She pushed me aside, her strength surprising.

When I moved only half a step, Killian caught my arm

and pulled me back some more. "What happened, Shane?" he asked, his voice low.

I opened my mouth, but nothing came out. Did I even know what had happened?

More footsteps echoed in the infirmary. Thea and Almae arrived. They took one look at Raika, and without hesitating, took over. They stood beside the vampire then hovered their hands over Raika's body, using their magic to find any wound or injury.

As far as I knew, there was none.

The only thing consoling me right now was the fact that I could hear Raika's heart beating and her breathing. She didn't seem to be in any danger, though that had been scary as hell.

"Bring a washcloth and water," Almae told the other female vampire. I had seen her a couple of times and didn't remember her name. The vampire nodded and headed to a storage room where all the supplies were located. Then she turned to me. "How are you?"

I opened my mouth again. Closed it. Swallowed, my throat parched and hurting. "I don't care about me," I finally said, my voice rough. "I care about her."

Lavinia stepped up to me and offered me a bottle of water. Where had she gotten this? I didn't care. I took the bottle and chugged the water.

The vampire came back and handed the washcloth to Thea and Almae.

"Thank you, Meredith," Almae said. That was her name.

The three of them dampened the washcloth and cleaned the soot from Raika's skin. Raika let out a long sigh, as if the chilliness in the washcloths was a balm to her hot skin. Even from the edge of the bed, I still could feel the heat radiating from her body, though it was much better now.

"Let me look at you," Meredith said.

I frowned. "Why?"

She held my wrists and extended my arms. I inhaled sharpy as I took in the red, angry skin on my arms. Thankfully, my apprehension toward Raika and the adrenaline from the moment had prevented me from feeling any pain, and my healing had already kicked in.

Meredith pressed her lips tight. "Do you want anything to speed your healing up? Or for pain, perhaps?"

I shook my head and turned away from her. "So?" I took a step closer to Thea and Almae. "How is she?"

Thea placed a washcloth on Raika's forehead. "She's fine ... for now."

"For now?" What the hell did that mean?

"Tell us what happened." Almae pulled a thin white blanket up to Raika's chest.

This time, I inhaled deeply, pushed through the haziness in my mind, and told them what had happened. I had taken her to the lake, proposed to her, she said yes, we kissed, and she erupted into fire.

Lavinia pressed her hand over her mouth. "You're engaged," she whispered.

At the same time, Thea nodded. "As I thought. It's the dragon's magic. It's acting faster than we predicted. It's spreading and taking over her darkfire."

I crossed my arms. "What does that mean?"

A soft moan came from the bed and Raika took a long breath. I stepped to her side and caught her hand in mine. It was hot, but not unbearably so. I leaned closer to her. "Hey, how are you?"

She blinked, taking another breath. "Like I was run over by a truck." She started sitting up in bed. Meredith and I helped her and put more pillows behind her back. Raika glanced around. "What happen—?" Her eyes went wide. "Fire," she whispered. I nodded. Horror filled her eyes. "Did I hurt you?"

I almost chuckled. Only her to care about others at a time like this. "No, you didn't. But you gave me quite the scare."

She pulled the blanket away, taking in her destroyed clothes. "By the moon ..."

Thea and Almae stood on the other side of the bed. "Raika, what did you feel before the fire took over?" Almae asked.

Raika's skin already had a reddish hue to it, but somehow, the red in her cheeks deepened. "I was with Shane, so ..."

Thea nodded. "Magic is linked to emotions. Since the dragon's magic is still unstable, strong emotion will trigger it."

"How ...?" I shut my mouth, not wanting to say the words, but curious. "How isn't she dead right now?"

"Because the dragon's magic is becoming a part of her," Thea said. "The fire won't burn her, though it'll probably burn everything else."

"These powers will only grow," Almae said. "We can make an elixir for you that will slow it down, and perhaps it'll help so you don't explode every time something happens."

"I would appreciate that," Raika said.

"We also should schedule some training," Thea added. "With training, you might have more control and eventually not need the elixir."

Raika nodded. "That sounds good too."

Almae rested a hand on Raika's legs. "For now, we would

like to keep you here. Just until we make the elixir and we're sure it works."

Raika looked at me, agony stamped in her beautiful eyes. "I wouldn't want to hurt my family or friends, or burn down the village." She sighed. "I'll stay here for as long as is needed."

My brows curled down. I didn't like the idea of Raika staying here. I would probably stay with her, which meant I would have to ask Rue to watch Minsi and Tyren.

"Stay here, then," Thea said. "Rest, sleep, recharge. If you feel anything happening, let Meredith know. She knows what to do when things get out of control."

Meredith gave Raika a reassuring smile. Although, what would she do if things got out of control? If she hurt Raika, she would lose an arm, if not her head.

I smoothed a hand over my face and let out a long breath. This was my fear and protectiveness talking. No one would hurt Raika.

"We'll work on the elixir," Almae said. "We'll be back as soon as we have it." She looked at Lavinia. "Want to help us?"

Lavinia nodded. "I'll be there in a minute." Thea and Almae walked out of the room and Lavinia squealed. "You two are engaged?"

With a smile, Raika looked at the ring on her finger. Thankfully, it hadn't been damaged like her clothes had. Her smile widened when she looked at me, and my heart lurched.

Killian slapped my shoulder. "Congratulations."

At that moment, I forced myself to push the thought of Raika on fire away from my mind, and focused on what had happened moments before and our promising future together.

Lavinia pulled a chair and sat beside Raika's bed. "So ...

tell me all your plans. Big or small wedding? Beach, country, ballroom? White or beige dress?"

Lavinia went on, distracting Raika so she wouldn't think of the dragon's magic and how she could hurt any of us if she lost control. I was grateful for that.

2

RAIKA

WHILE LAVINIA DISTRACTED ME TALKING ABOUT THE WEDDING, Shane went to the village to get me clothes and other things. I didn't want a big wedding, and it would probably be at the center of the village if we still lived here. My dress would probably be a different color ... not white, not beige. Maybe gray? Could one get married in black? Seriously, I didn't think those fluffy, white dresses were for me.

But as I thought about the wedding, I knew it wouldn't happen anytime soon. I had to master the dragon magic, and we still had to deal with Paimon. I couldn't focus on my future, knowing my father was out there, vying for more and more power.

Right before noon, Shane came back with a bagful of my things. Meredith showed me to the bathroom inside the infirmary. I stepped under the warm water and felt cold. I knew I was still hot to the touch, but it seemed now everything else felt cold against me. I made the water as hot as I could and then rethought it. I quickly switched to cold water, the coldest I could endure, and washed myself like that.

As I washed my hair, I sighed. One moment, I was kissing Shane, excited about his proposal, and then, I exploded.

And I blacked out.

Waking in the infirmary had been disconcerting. Why were my skin and hair intact and my clothes and shoes weren't? How could I endure the dragon's magic? I wasn't a dragon or a dragon shifter.

It was a neat trick, but an unwelcome one. A beautiful, majestic dragon had died for this magic.

I wish I could give it back, but magic couldn't be returned to a dead dragon.

I sighed again. If there was a way to transfer this magic to a dragon or a dragon shifter, Kaz would have told us.

I finished my shower, brushed my damp hair, and put on a pair of ripped jeans and a tank top.

I walked out of the bathroom on bare feet and halted.

Minsi, Tyren, Rue, and Jay had brought us lunch. My heart squeezed seeing the worried looks on their faces.

Minsi ran to me, wrapping her arms round my waist. I stared at Shane. *What do I do?* I asked with my eyes. He smiled at me. What if I hurt her? What if the fire came back? I knew Meredith could stop me, but what if she wasn't fast enough?

I allowed myself to embrace Minsi, then I pulled back, held her hand, and walked to the bed. Before I could take two steps, Jay halted in front of me.

"I'm sorry," he said, his voice breaking.

I stared at him. What had happened? Shane looked at me and sighed. "It's okay, Jay. She's fine now."

"It's not fine." Jay lowered his head. "Shane came to me first and I ... the infirmary isn't ready, but also I ..." He sighed. "I panicked. I—I saw you all orange and you looked dead. I thought I would mess it up instead of making it better."

If I wasn't afraid of hurting him, I would have hugged him. As it was, I touched my hand to his arm. "It's all right, Jay. If you didn't feel ready, I'm glad you said as much to Shane."

"What kind of healer turns a patient away? I turned you away."

"You need more experience and confidence in yourself." I pressed a finger to his chest, right above his heart. "More trust in here."

He shook his head. "I'm not good enough for this."

I was too tired to argue about this. "Jay, I'm fine. You're fine, and one day you'll be an amazing healer. Just don't give up."

Meredith emerged from her office. "Jay, why don't you train with me?" His eyes sparked. "Come into my office, let's talk."

Jay barely wasted another second with us. He bolted after Meredith and I shot her a thankful look. She smiled at me before closing her office door.

I resumed my trek to the bed, where I gently pushed Minsi toward Shane, and hopped over the mattress.

"Bringing them here is risky," I muttered.

"They wanted to see you," he said.

"Then at least keep them back."

Tyren frowned. "We're not afraid."

My heart almost broke in half. "I know, and I'm thankful for that, but this magic is strong and stubborn. I still don't know how to control it. I don't want to hurt you."

He crossed his arms. "I know you won't hurt us."

His confidence in me was reassuring, but I didn't give in to all of it. Shane shot me a just-enjoy-this-moment look, so I let out a long breath.

They all sat in chairs around my bed, their plates resting on their laps as we ate Rue's lasagna. Halfway through the meal, I brought the napkin to my lips.

Minsi inhaled deeply.

Tyren pointed at me. His eyes bugged and he looked from me to Shane. "You proposed?"

Shane ran a hand through his hair. "This morning. Right before Raika fell sick. Sorry I didn't get a chance to tell you." He put his plate aside. "I was planning on telling everyone tonight at dinner so we could celebrate ..."

"But I've ruined it," I added.

Shane frowned. "It wasn't your fault."

I looked at Minsi and Tyren. "Are you two okay with this? If not, just say it. We'll—"

"Are you crazy?" Tyren asked.

"Tyren!" Shane snapped. "What the hell?"

"Sorry." Tyren's shoulders sagged a little. "I didn't mean it like that. It's just ..." He looked at Minsi, Shane, then at me. "You're part of this family. You have been for some time now. We are more than okay with it."

My heart warmed, a huge smile spreading over my lips. "That is ..." Tears brimmed in my eyes. "It's just that I would never impose on you, if you didn't want this too. But thank you. That means a lot to me." I waved at my eyes.

Shane shot to his feet, returning to my side. "Calm down. Take deep breaths." He did it with me. One, two, three deep inhales and slow exhales. "After you learn how to control the dragon magic, we can celebrate. For now, we should try to avoid all that."

He looked at Tyren, who gave him a short nod.

We finished eating and Rue showed us the chocolate candy bars she had brought for dessert. "I didn't have time to make something, so chocolate it is."

I unwrapped a milky way. "This is perfect. Thank you." I glanced at all of them. "Thanks for coming and having lunch with me."

We ate the chocolate, talked about school and their tasks for the day, then Rue escorted the kids out. Jay had long been gone and we hadn't even seen him leaving.

Although I would spend the night here, I wanted to ask Shane to go home. The kids needed him and we had abandoned them so much in the last month. It all had been necessary, but I disliked it.

For now, I enjoyed the fact he was snuggled in bed with me. "You must be tired. Go to sleep."

I laid my head on his shoulder. "I'm not that tired."

He kissed my forehead and smooth his hand down my back, tucking me even closer to him. "Just try."

I didn't fight it, and that proved that this whole ordeal had indeed zapped my energy and I needed rest. I closed my eyes, inhaled his familiar musky scent, and drifted off to sleep.

***

WHEN I WOKE UP, SHANE WASN'T IN BED. PANIC STOLE MY breath, and I had to orient myself ... I was in the infirmary.

Shane stood before the long window on the other side of the room.

I stared at him for a minute, always impressed by how handsome and strong he was. Today, he wore fitted jeans and a dark green Henley shirt that hugged his hard shoulders and arms perfectly.

The afternoon sun bathed him in a golden light, and for a moment, he seemed like a wolf god.

With a sly smile, he turned to me. "Watching me again, hm?"

Heat spread to my cheeks. "You caught me."

He walked toward me. "Keep staring. I don't mind. But I might stare too."

I ran a hand through my messy hair. It was worse than a rat's nest. "How about you wait until I don't feel so messy?"

He sat beside me, facing me, his eyes on mine. "How are you feeling?"

I was still a little tired, as if the fire had incinerated my energy. I was also bored, though my stay here had barely begun. I was worried about hurting others. Maybe we should have a tent outside in an open field, with some kind of moat around me, so even if I burned and burned the tent, the fire wouldn't spread and I couldn't hurt anyone. And I also felt the magic within me. I couldn't explain it, but sometimes it felt like an oily snake swimming through my veins, wrapping around my bones, making itself comfortable and claiming my body as its home.

The knot in Shane's forehead deepened. "Has it flared up since this morning?"

"Only when Tyren made me emotional earlier, but you noticed before I did." Thank goodness. If it weren't for Shane, I'm not sure what would have happened.

He held my hand in his. "Soon, Thea and Almae will come back with your elixir."

"They are still working on it," Killian said as he entered the infirmary. "Lavinia is there with them. They have been there nonstop since this morning."

That made me feel bad. I hated making work and trouble

to others. "Tell them to take a break, or the rest of the day off. I think we can manage a day or two without it." I had no idea if that was true, but I wanted to believe it.

Shane frowned again. "I bet they want to do it."

Killian nodded. "They love this kind of stuff. They are doing it because they enjoy it."

That made me feel a little better. "Thanks." Killian shrugged, but his expression darkened. "What is it?"

He shook his head. "I talked to Drake. He apologized for not coming to see you, but with the tension with the demons, he's busier than ever."

"What did he tell you?" Shane asked, his tone somber.

"There's no progress," Killian said. "The demon hunters amassed most of their forces and searched the entire country and Canada, and they can't find Paimon ... or Rotgar, or Ivy."

A wave of apprehension at the sound of my sister's name seized my chest. I pushed that feeling aside. "If he's gathering an army, shouldn't it be easy to find?"

"It seems that way, doesn't it?" Killian asked. "But he has some good hiding tricks."

I wished I could help Killian and Drake and the demon hunters, but Paimon had been smart. He had never revealed his plan to me or where I could hear it. I hadn't realized that until I was free. Right now, I was of no help.

"Next meeting Lord Drake calls, let me know," Shane said. He glanced at me. "We might stay out of the fight, but I would like to be kept in the loop."

"Wait." I sat straighter. "You want to stay out of the fight?"

A wave of tension rolled around the room. "I'll ..." He pointed to the door across the room. "Yeah." He zipped out with his super vampire speed without saying goodbye.

I stared at Shane, not understanding. "What do you mean we'll stay out of the fight?"

He squared his shoulders. "With your powers, it might not be a good idea. You could lose it in the middle of the battle and burn our people. It's too risky until you have control."

"With the elixir and proper training, it won't be," I countered.

"We might not have time for training. We don't know when Paimon plans to attack."

"He's in hiding, and he might be unstable like I am. He might need time to get a handle on the dragon magic. That should give me time to train."

"That is a big if."

"What do you want me to do, then? Sit here and twiddle my thumbs while our friends march into battle?"

Shane's jaw ticked. "I want you to be safe."

"While Paimon is out there, trying to take the underworld back, I'm not safe. No one is."

"That's why the others will deal with him."

I let out a long breath. "Shane, please, don't do this. Don't be a chauvinist and—"

"I'm being protective of the people I love."

I shook my head. "I'm not weak. I can defend myself and others. We can't sit this one out."

He shot to his feet and the chair almost fell back. "I ... I can't go through it again, Raika. I can't. I thought you died twice, and then you caught fire in front of my eyes not even eight hours ago. I can't see you in any more danger. My soul can't take it."

I knew where he was coming from, but it wasn't fair. He didn't get to choose for me. Besides ... "You do realize I have the same powers as Paimon now, don't you? I might be the only one able to stop him." His eyes widened as if he hadn't considered that. "You can't keep me from this fight."

He clenched his hands into fists and his jaw hardened. "Think about Minsi and Tyren … and me. We need you and we need you here. Not fighting a war that already has thousands of people signed up for."

I couldn't believe I was hearing this. "Shane—"

"No!" He almost shouted and I flinched. "I won't hear another damn word about this."

He spun on his heel, marching away.

I stayed seated in bed, staring at the door long after he left, confused and alone.

3

RAIKA

I couldn't believe Shane had left. That was not how you fixed an argument. Would he do that every time we disagreed on something? I didn't like being upset at him, and I was sure he didn't like being mad at me.

I started moving from the bed, intent on following him and making him talk to me so we could fix whatever rift this was and make up.

Meredith walked into the room from her office. "Good, you're awake. I would like to check you out."

Shit. I sat back down. Maybe it was for the best if I gave Shane a few minutes. He needed to clear his head and let go of his anger before we were able to talk.

Meredith came to the bed's side, beginning her examination. She told me to relax while she listened for my heart and breathing. She checked my temperature: higher than was normal for a wolf, and we already ran higher than humans, but not overly so.

"The dragon's magic seems to be quiet," she said. "For now."

That wasn't reassuring. Then again, I knew it wasn't supposed to be. Vampires weren't known for their gentle nature. Meredith would tell me how it was without any sugar-coating.

"Thea said that if I start losing control, you can do something about it," I said. "What is it?"

One corner of her lips tugged up. "I'll tell you some other time." She patted my leg and walked away.

I looked out the window. The sun was already descending, though since it was almost summer, we still had a few of hours of sunlight.

I reconsidered going after Shane, but I thought of the village and our wolves. There was a reason I was being kept here—so I didn't hurt anyone if I lost control. I couldn't go after Shane and end up hurting others. Especially because something told me we would argue more before making up, and if I got angry, who knew what could happen?

I stayed put, bored out of my mind. I laid my back on the pillows propped up on the bed, picked up my phone, and started browsing books. I wasn't in the mood to read, but I could see the new releases of this past month and choose what I would like to read.

Footsteps approached and a moment later, Thea, Almae, and Lavinia walked in.

Thea lifted her hand, showing me the rectangular box she was holding. "Here it is." She walked to the bed, put the box over the side table, and picked up one of many vials inside. "

"We used the flower from the mountain," Lavinia announced, sounding a little too eager. "Don't worry, it seems totally safe, and it has a calming effect, which is perfect for this."

Thea nodded, handing me the vial. "It should help stabilize the dragon magic."

I took it and turned it around in my hand, the yellow liquid shining almost golden. "What happens when we train? Won't this make it harder for me to access the magic?"

"This elixir won't last long." Almae gestured to the box. "That's why there are so many. You should drink one every four to six hours, depending on how you're feeling and your emotions."

I frowned. "So the idea is to schedule training between doses?"

Thea nodded. "Exactly."

"You should drink it," Lavinia urged me.

I uncorked the vial and an acrid scent reached my nose. "Any side effects I should know about?"

"We did everything we could so there wouldn't be any," Almae said. That was good. If only every medicine out there was like that.

I held my breath and downed the elixir. A burning sensation traveled down my throat and I hissed.

"Here." Lavinia picked up the glass of water from the side table, offering it to me.

I drank two big gulps and sighed.

The three witches watched me carefully, making me feel like I was under a microscope.

"Feel anything?" Thea asked.

I frowned. "No—" I gasped as my insides relaxed on their own accord. It was like a balm had descended upon the dragon's magic, calming it, and I could breathe again. "I think it's working."

Meredith stepped forward and took my temperature. "It's lower."

Almae smiled. "That's a good sign."

"But remember, it won't last long," Thea reminded me. "If we made it stronger, it might have upset your stomach or worse. Follow the directions, or whenever you feel like you're losing it."

I nodded, realizing I had drunk one. "So, no training for now."

Thea shook her head. "We'll start tomorrow morning, after your first dose of the day starts fading."

"For now, stay here, have a good night's rest." Almae squeezed my arm gently. "You need it."

Thea and Almae promised to come check on me later, before they retreated for the night, but they told me that if I needed them, I could call on them at any time, even in the middle of the night. They left, but Lavinia stayed.

She pulled a chair closer to my bed. "How are you?"

"Bored. Tired of resting," I confessed. I knew this was important, though. Everything that was happening was new; no one had any experience with it. We couldn't make any mistakes or others could get hurt. "But I understand."

"I can get you some books from the library. Tell me which ones. And I can also order something special for dinner. Tell me what you want."

I smiled at her, happy she was my friend. I asked for a book about dragons. Now that I had all this power inside me, I wanted to understand it. As for dinner, I asked for pepperoni pizza. Plain and simple.

Lavinia laughed. "Of course. I might bring it over and stay for dinner too."

I shrugged. "I don't mind. Invite Killian too. The more, the merrier."

She frowned. "Speaking of that, where's Shane?"

I clicked my tongue. "We had a small argument and he stomped away from here."

Her eyes bugged. "That's unlike him."

"I know, and that makes me more upset." I smoothed the blanket over my legs. "Actually, I'm more upset that I couldn't go after him." It had been a couple of hours since he left. I had hoped he would have calmed down and be back by now.

"Do you want me to find him?"

"No, it's okay. He'll come when he's ready to talk."

Lavinia stayed with me for a few more minutes, then she went to find me some books and order my pizza.

I lay back on the pillows, again bored and alone.

But it wasn't for long.

I felt the tug in my heart and heard his footsteps before he opened the infirmary's door and walked in.

"Shane," I whispered.

4

SHANE

As soon as I ran from that infirmary, I let my wolf out. My clothes ripped apart and fell on the castle's pristine floors. I dashed past vampires and witches, and they all stepped out of my way before I ran over them. Right now, my anger burned like the sun and I needed to snuff it out.

Outside, I crossed the back garden and entered the forest.

I aimlessly ran for over an hour. Then I chased a squirrel and a deer. Killian appeared at some point and finished off the deer I had been chasing. He ran with me a little.

When we finally stopped, he asked, "Do you want to talk?"

I shook my head. "Do you want to be alone?"

I nodded.

"All right. Then I'll go back to the castle. You know where to find me."

He zipped away with his super speed, and I was alone again. I ran another hour before the anger and anxiety fizzled out.

I slowed down, trying to quell the war raging in my

thoughts and with my emotions. I wanted to be a supportive partner, but how did I keep Raika safe? I couldn't control her —I would never do that—but sitting back and watching her fight, knowing this next one would be to the death...

If she didn't kill Paimon, he would kill her. And this time, it wouldn't be a trick. It would be real.

I couldn't go through that again.

I made my way back to the castle.

Lord Drake was waiting for me outside the tree line, with a pair of jeans and shirt folded in his arms.

I stopped in front of him and shifted back. Without a word, he handed me the clothes, and I dressed.

It wasn't normal for him to show up like this. "What happened?"

"Shane, I value all you've done for my coven. I trust you and I admired you, and for those reasons, I'll get directly to the point: Raika might be the only one who can stop Paimon."

I cursed under my breath. So he had figured that out too? "I know," I gritted out.

Drake nodded. "I thought you would."

Raika realized it first and that had been such a shock, it had sent me spiraling. I wasn't stupid. I think I had always known what it would come down to the moment the dragon's damn power split and half of it went into Raika.

"All I want is to keep my family safe."

"I know," Drake said. "I understand your feelings."

"If that means staying back, then that's what I want," I went on. "However, I know it is not that simple."

"Shane, if Raika doesn't help, we'll certainly lose, and countless more lives will be claimed until we find a way of killing him. With Raika's help, we could end this—now."

"Are you one hundred percent sure Raika is the only one who can kill him?"

"I met with Hadrian, Erin, Rey, and a few others. Everyone thinks that with the dragon magic, Raika and Paimon are each other's only match." He clasped my shoulder. "I know what we are asking of you and Raika is a lot, but be assured, we'll be there every step of the way. We won't let anything happen to her."

I knew they would do their best, but even I had failed to protect her before. I didn't want to risk a third time.

I let out a long breath, my muscles tense. "I want to tell you all to fuck off ... with all due respect." Drake's lips twitched up. "But I think this is something Raika has to decide for herself." As much as it pained me to admit that.

Drake dropped his arm. "Wise words."

"I'll talk to her." It was high time I went back to her so we could finish our conversation. "I'll let you know what she says."

"Thank you."

"Don't thank me yet." I hoped Raika would say no, but I already knew her answer. She had made it clear earlier.

We both walked back to the castle. Drake headed to his office—the vampire lord never stopped—and I turned into the infirmary.

I paused at the door, took a long breath, and pushed it open.

Raika was still in bed, the blanket over her legs, and her eyes on me.

"Shane," she whispered.

A tug came from my chest, so hard, so deep, I almost bent over. Slowly, I entered the room, closed the door behind me, and approached her bed with my tail between my legs. I was still seething on the inside, but for her, I would try to keep my anger in check.

Raika crossed her arms and a knot formed between her brows. She had every right to be mad at me.

"I'm sorry I walked out on you." I halted at the bed's footboard. "I just ... I was losing it and I needed to take my sorry ass for a run."

She took in my shirt and jeans. "I see you have different clothes on."

I nodded. "Lord Drake gave them to me after my run."

"Lord Drake?"

"Yeah, we spoke."

"Did you yell at him too?"

I flinched. "I don't think I yelled at you, but I did raise my voice and almost lost it, and for that, I apologize."

"What else?"

"I messed up something else?" I thought for a second. "Tell me and then I'll fix it."

One corner of her lips moved up, but she smoothed her expression and stared at me deadpan. "We should finish the conversation we started earlier."

"I agree." I wrapped my hands around the footboard. "You were saying you might be the only one who can stop Paimon."

"Right."

"Drake and others think so too."

Her eyebrows shot high. "He told you that?"

I nodded. "He said he won't force us, you, to act, but he promised that if you did, he and the others will be there to protect you."

"And how do you feel about that?"

I pressed my lips tight. "I hate it. I don't want you to go

anywhere." The tug in my chest was back. "If I could, I would lock you away and not let you leave, ever, just to keep you safe ... but I know that is my overprotectiveness talking, the bond making me go crazy every time I think of you in danger. I mean it when I say I don't want to go through that pain ever again ... but then we might as well just give up living."

"What are you saying?"

I exhaled, my nostrils flaring. "That I'm not a selfish, stupid grump who will hold you back. If you want to fight Paimon, that is your choice. I'll support whatever you choose."

She gave me a side eye. "Is this a trick?"

I let out a hollow chuckle. "No trick. I mean it. You're strong and I believe in you. If you're the only one who can stop Paimon and you want to do it, then I'll be the first one to cheer you on."

Her shoulders relaxed. "What changed?"

"Nothing. I just ... thought a lot. You're mine, but you're also your own person. You should make your own decisions. Plus, I don't want to fight with you. I see the logic in the decision, I see why we have to do this, even if I don't like it."

She pushed away from the pillows. "So, if I say I want to do it ...?"

Again, I exhaled. "I'll stop arguing about it and I'll do it with you."

She crawled over the bed, stood on her knees right at the footboard, and wrapped her arms around my neck. "Thank you."

I groaned. "I can't promise I'll be sensible all the time. I'll protest here and there. I can't help it."

She grinned at me. "I'll take that."

Dear moon, she was beautiful. I wound my arms around

her waist and pulled her to me. "You drive me insane. In all the senses of the word."

"Ditto," she muttered. She tugged on my neck and I bent into her. I closed my mouth around hers, kissing her.

It didn't matter if we didn't agree. It didn't matter that we fought. What mattered was that we were willing to meet halfway and make it work. Because we were meant for each other. Because she was my fated mate. She was mine.

And I was hers.

Raika bit my lower lip and pure desire took hold of me. With a growl, I moved. Raining kisses down her neck, I rounded the footboard, laid her down on the mattress, and crawled over her. I pressed my body against hers, her breasts squished against my chest, her hips lined with mine, her legs open and around my waist to let me get as close as I could ... and I growled again.

My hard-on became painful against my pants.

I brought my lips back to Raika's and claimed her mouth, while I slipped my hand down her breast, across her belly, and inside her pants. I touched her center and Raika hissed, her back arching.

"Want more?" I asked against her lips.

"Always," she breathed. "With you, anything, always."

I growled and rubbed at her clit.

Raika's body heated up. Startled, I pulled back and stared at her orange skin. "Raika?"

"Shit," she muttered. Her hands shook. "I'm losing it. Quick. The vial." She pointed to a box on the side table. I jumped off the bed, reached for the box, opened it, and grabbed a vial from inside. I uncorked it for her. Raika snatched it from me and drank it all in one gulp.

She lay back, her breathing hard, her chest moving

rapidly, her eyes dazed. The vial rolled from her hand and crashed to the floor.

Panic seized my chest. "Raika?"

"I'm fine," she whispered. "The elixir helped. It's coming back down."

I ran a hand through my hair. Damn, I shouldn't have done that. I shouldn't have kissed her or touched her. I knew what could happened, and yet, lost in my own desire for her, I had forgotten.

"I'm sorry."

She propped herself up on her elbows. "Why? Because of this? It isn't your fault." She reached for me, but I only took a step away. "Shane, don't you dare withdraw from me now. We might not be able to get hot and heavy, but please, don't leave me alone."

Shit. That was what she read in my action. "I'm not leaving you alone. I'll never leave you. I'm just trying to protect you."

She sat up, crossed her legs, and patted the bed. I sat down. "I love it that you want to protect me. I do. It's ... sexy." She entwined our fingers together. "As long as you stay with me."

I brought her hand up and kissed the top. "Always."

"Aw, you two made up." Lavinia's voice rang from the infirmary's door. "That's sweet."

She walked in, pushing a fancy metal cart with plates, cups, beverages, and ... pizza? Killian followed her in and closed the door behind them.

"Are we having a party?" I asked, confused.

Lavinia shrugged. "If you want, I can come up with an idea for a party right here, right now."

Raika chuckled. "But did you bring my book?"

"Booksss," she said, emphasizing the s. She gestured to the bottom shelf of the metal cart, where there was a pile of leather-bound books.

"You're a saint." Raika made grabby hands.

Lavinia snorted. "So far from that." She picked up the first book and handed it to Raika.

"What's that about?" I asked.

Raika showed me the cover. *The Real History of Dragons and Dragon Shifters.*

"Apparently, Raika asked for books on dragons, and Lavinia wanted us to bring all of them," Killian said, in a mad-teasing tone. "By the way, we didn't. There are too many books on the subject in the library."

"Good, then it means I have a lot to learn." Raika cracked open the book.

"Nah." Lavinia picked the book up and put it on the side table. "I was letting you have a preview. Now it's dinnertime." She held up the plates while Killian cut the pizza.

"You know you don't have to eat with us," I said. The vampires didn't need to eat like us. Blood was enough for them, but sometimes they did, whenever the witches were having a celebration or party.

Lavinia handed me a plate with a huge pizza slice. "Pizza is too good to pass up."

Killian nodded. "True."

I glanced from them to Raika. We had made up, our friends were here with us, and we were having a pizza party. Right now, everything was okay. And that was all that mattered.

I took a big bite of my pizza and enjoyed the moment.

I was sure it wouldn't last.

5

RAIKA

AFRAID OF CALLING THE FIRE AGAIN, SHANE PULLED ANOTHER bed in the room and placed it beside mine. This way, we were close, but not touching.

Which made me sad. I was growing used to sleeping with our bodies tangled together.

I had asked him to go back home and stay with the kids, but he insisted the kids understood. And Rue was with them.

When we woke up, Shane went to find us breakfast. I took a quick shower and put on a pair of leather leggings and a crop top, along with my wedge black boots. Then, I took another dose of the elixir and Meredith examined me.

"The elixir seems to be working," she said as she took my temperature. "Still high for a wolf, but nothing to worry about."

When Shane returned, he pushed a cart brimming with food: bacon, eggs, toast, pancakes, juice, milk, and coffee.

"How many people are eating with us?" I joked.

Shane served a plate with a little of everything and

handed it to me. "You're starting your training today. You need energy."

"Right, but this is too much."

He sat on the bed, holding a plate. "Just eat, smartass."

We ate in silence. I had to admit ... bacon, eggs, toast, and pancakes were such a common thing, but whoever was the cook in this castle was exceptional. He, or she, made it all taste like a piece of heaven. When I felt better, I would have to express my thanks.

"What time is your training?" Shane asked after swallowing a big bite of his pancake, drenched in syrup.

"I just took the elixir, and I'm supposed to drink it every four to six hours, depending on how I feel. So maybe in four hours?"

Shane nodded. "I would like to be there."

"I would love that, but don't you have other things to do? Like check on the kids? And maybe on everyone else? I don't want you to pause everything because of me."

"You're more important."

I smiled. "I love hearing that, but you know how the pack wolves can be. Until a few weeks ago, some of them weren't so keen on having you as an alpha, then me as your mate ... I don't want to have another problem with them. Not so soon, at least."

Shane shoved a forkful of pancakes in his mouth, his brows dipped low. After chewing and swallowing, he finally said, "Fine. I'll do alpha stuff while you train."

"As soon as it's over, I'll text you. You can bring me another delicious thing to eat then."

He groaned. "Are you going to start a fan club for the chef?"

"I just might." I chuckled. "Is he handsome?"

Shane stiffened. He caught my teasing, but didn't relax. "When you're better, I'll introduce you to him."

Hm, he probably wasn't handsome or Shane wouldn't offer to take me to him.

We finished eating, put everything aside, and snuggled in the bed, making time until it was time for my training. Our backs on the bed's headboard, with pillows under us, I propped a heavy book on our legs and started reading it while Shane messed with his phone.

Dragon History 101 depicted the little we knew about dragons, and from what I had learned, it was wrong, since this book also mentioned dragons had gone extinct almost a thousand years ago, and dragon shifters were gone as well.

This book elaborated on how dragon shifters came to be. The story told of a human who, instead of hunting the dragons, tried to help them. In doing so, this human, a young woman named Alice, was also hunted by other humans—and the supernaturals who wanted the dragon's powers. In an ambush, she was fatally injured. To save Alice, one of the dragons, Galzrer, gave her half of his magic—and performed a ritual to have the human's body accept those powers. Alice became the first dragon shifter, the most powerful of all. After her death, she was revered as a deity and praised by the entire dragon shifter and dragon races.

Shane lowered his phone. "Anything interesting?"

"I guess." I flipped the page and saw a crude family tree of Alice and her offspring. Under the graphic was a short text:

When a dragon shifter has a child with another species, that child becomes 100 percent dragon shifter. However, in rare cases, if the child is born from a strong supernatural, she may retain their powers too.

"Very interesting," I muttered.

I continued reading the book, skimming the pages, but nowhere did it elaborated about when the dragon magic was stolen, or split in two.

One thought stayed with me: Galzrer had given Alice half of his magic and performed a ritual. Then she became a dragon shifter. I had half of a dragon's magic. If we performed this ritual, would I become a dragon shifter?

I frowned. I was already a half-wolf shifter, and half demon. I didn't want to be another supernatural. Hopefully, no one would bring that up or perform the ritual without me knowing.

Shane texted Dom and Tyren, already starting whatever was on the agenda for today.

Thea and Almae entered the infirmary and greeted us a short time later.

"Are you ready?" Thea asked.

Dear moon, I hoped I was. I nodded.

THE SUV ROLLED THROUGH THE SMOOTH, NEWLY RENOVATED road from DuMoir Castle to the Silverblood Estate, and the road to the Silver Moon Academy.

"Look," Almae said from my side in the backseat. Lavinia sat on her other side.

I glanced ahead and inhaled sharply as the wrought iron gates came into view, the academy's emblem in silver in the center. Stone pillars flanked the gates, and walls went to the right and left as far as the eye could see.

As we approached, the gates opened, revealing more road and half a mile ahead, a beautiful building.

"Welcome to the Silver Moon Academy," Thea said from the passenger seat with a smile.

"It's very special to us," Elisa said. She was the one driving us.

"It looks enchanting," I said, in awe.

"No pun intended?" Lavinia teased. I shot her a you-know-that-was-intended look.

We drove to the front of the academy, where another witch I didn't know waited for us. She was dressed in a beautiful gown. I looked down at my leggings and blouse. Maybe I should have dressed up. Nope, that wasn't me. They would have to deal with my style.

Elisa turned off the engine and we hopped out of the SUV. The sun was already too warm for my taste, but the day was green and smelled of fresh flowers, which made me content.

"Good morning," she said with a bright smile.

"Good morning," Thea said, approaching the witch. "Mila, this is Raika." She gestured to me. "Raika, this is Mila. She's been helping us here at the academy."

Mila and I shook hands.

"Nice to meet you," she said.

"You too."

"Mila, why don't we do a quick tour of the main building before we start the training?" Thea suggested.

"Of course," Mila said. "Please, follow me."

We all followed Mila inside the academy. My mouth hung open the entire tour as we walked through the majestic foyer, wide hallways, fancy offices and meetings room, and a large media room with over two hundred theater-like chairs. As we walked, Mila explained that this building had actually been a semi-destroyed mansion they had found. They bought it, fixed it, and built around it. On the other side of the courtyard, construction was ongoing, though classes had officially started in January this year, seven months ago. Right now, the first thirty-two witches attending the academy were on summer break and back with their covens.

We exited through a large side door into a neatly manicured garden with white, pink, and red roses, and continued down a narrow stone path until we found another large, stone building.

"This is our special training facility," Mila said as she opened one panel of the double doors.

We walked in and stopped shy of the entrance. I frowned, taking in the place. The entire building was one gigantic room with high ceilings and no windows. An unfinished white circle was painted around the entire room.

"I thought you said this is special," I said.

Thea nodded. "It's special because in here, no magic can hurt us." She opened her arms wide. "The walls, floors, and ceiling are enchanted so even if you burst into fire and lose control, you won't exploded beyond this building. It'll even counteract your magic, and smother it if needed."

My brows lifted. "That's great. But what about you? You'll be in here with me."

"There are two safety mechanisms in this room." Elisa pointed to the thick, white line on the floor near us. I followed it with my eyes. It was a giant witch's circle that went around the perimeter; however, it wasn't closed. "We can quickly close the circle and contain whatever is inside."

"Or ..." Almae walked farther into the room, pointing to a thick line on the floor in one of the corners. There were several of those spread throughout the room. "We can raise these walls. They have the same spell as the rest of the building. Technically, if we hide behind them, we'll be protected."

"Technically?" I didn't like the sound of that.

"We've tested it with our powers, but we haven't had anyone truly losing control of their magic in here yet," she explained.

I gulped. So I would be the first. Hopefully, it wouldn't happen. Hopefully, this training would be a breeze. Hopefully, I would master it in one day and be able to join the army against Paimon.

I rolled my shoulders. "All right. When do we start?"

"Right now." Thea stepped into the white circle. "Come."

She halted in the center of the room. I walked to her and stopped in front of her. The others remained outside the circle.

"What do you want me to do?"

"Let's start with your darkfire," Thea said. "Show me."

I spread my feet apart and focused. My darkfire was entwined with the dragon's magic now. It was hard distinguishing the two. I raised a hand and a ball of darkfire the size of an apple floated above my palm. I played with it, like I had done with Ivy. It became fluid and changed shapes: a dart, a ring, a cone, a whirlwind, and back to a ball with flickering flames.

"Good." Thea took four steps back. She stopped right behind one of marks on the floor, where she could raise a solid wall. "Now do the same with the dragon's magic."

I waved my hand and the darkfire disappeared. I inhaled deeply and looked within myself. Supposedly, dragon's magic was a kind of fire while it was still inside the dragon. But once it was taken, it became dark magic, much like darkfire. Inside of me, it felt like a river of fire, but when manifested, it looked like white flames.

I inhaled, feeling the fire moving through my veins. Now that it had been a few hours since I had taken the elixir, I could feel it stronger, deeper, and growing unstable.

This time, though, I knew what to do, what to expect. I had just learned how to control my darkfire. This wouldn't be different, would it?

The magic flowed to my fingertips and a flicker of flames surged above my open palm. I focused, called it again, and this time the flame held. It was the size of a closed fist, and the flames licked up to my head.

Feeling bold, I juggled the white flame from hand to hand a few times. Then I held it between my two open palms and made it bigger than my head. The heat brushed against my skin, but in a good way. The dragon's magic was such a part of me now, the heat didn't bother me.

I dropped my hands and let the fire go. "What now? Should I do it again?"

"Now, try one magic in each hand," Thea said.

Oh, that was new, and not something I had thought of before.

A knot formed between my brows as I focused. The darkfire came to me easily. It floated above my open palm. The dragon's magic was harder. Every time I thought I got a hold on it, the darkfire began slipping, and when I held the darkfire, the dragon's magic got away.

I let the darkfire go, took a deep breath, rolled my shoulders, and tried again.

And again, the darkfire was easy, but the dragon's magic was stubborn. It wanted exclusivity, as if it was the king of all magic. Perhaps it was, but if I didn't dominate it, then it would dominate me.

I groaned and tried again.

And again.

And again.

"This damn magic," I muttered, following with a string of curses.

"You know magic is emotional," Thea reminded me. "If you can't remain calm, it won't obey or it'll rebel."

I walked around the room, shaking my shoulders and arms, breathing deeply and trying to calm down. Though I had hoped this would go easy, I knew the reality was much different. Dragon magic was a lot harder and more powerful than darkfire. Of course it would fight me.

But I could do this. I just needed the right mindset.

After blowing off some steam, I came back to the center of the room. I closed my eyes, imagining myself in my happy place: a ragged couch where I sat beside Shane, Minsi, and Tyren. All of us squished together and smiling at each other. I let that image calm me, take over my mind, fill my heart.

I let out a long breath.

Then, I opened my eyes and tried again.

This time, though, I started with the dragon's magic. It took me a minute, but I conjured a small flame above my left palm. I held on to it for dear life as I split my focus, calling on a more familiar magic. The darkfire surged in my hand. It flickered, the dragon's fire flickered higher, as if trying to show off to the darkfire, but I concentrated on both. I was divided in two and each half of me controlled one different power.

I could do this.

I really could.

I inhaled and exhaled, making the bolts bigger. The dragon magic sparked, but I gritted my teeth. It took everything in me to make it stable, to make it behave. Sweat beaded my forehead as I made the bolts bigger. I held on for a moment, breathing hard, but still in control—barely. No, I had to get used to this. These two powers had to get used to being brought out together. They shared one body, one mind. My mind, and I was in control here.

Channeling, I played with the two bolts. I made the darkfire blink—one second it was there, the next it wasn't, and then it was again. Then I did it with the dragon's magic. The fire didn't disappear all the way, and when it came back, it was more unstable, pulling more of my energy.

I groaned and forced it into submission.

"Raika, that's enough for now," Thea said, her tone clipped.

I wanted to keep going. I wanted to do more, because I knew that once I let both magics go, it would take a lot more of me to bring them back. But I also knew Thea was right. I was getting exhausted and we had been at this for only an hour.

I exhaled and started dropping my hands, letting go of the magic. The bolts flickered, their flames touching. Instantly, my body heated up.

Red surrounded me.

I blacked out.

I SAT UP WITH A JERK, CONFUSED. WHAT HAPPENED? ONE moment, I had been in the training room with the witches and now ... I looked around.

Many faces stared back at me, their eyes grave—Thea, Almae, Lavinia, Elisa, Mila. Even Killian and Drake were here. And—

Directly to my right, holding my hand, was Shane.

I frowned, trying to connect the dots. Oh, shit. "I went up in fire again?"

Thea pressed a hand to my forehead. "Still hot. How are you feeling?"

"I'm ..." I paused and analyzed myself. My heart was racing, my skin felt warmer than usual, the two magics inside me were pushing against one another, but other than that, "I'm fine."

Thea's brows slammed down. "You gave us quite the scare."

Oh no. "Did I explode? Were you able to close me in? Was anyone hurt?" I glanced around again. The witches seemed fine. I let out a breath of relief, but I still felt bad about the situation. "I'm sorry I almost hurt you all."

"Don't worry about that, dear," Almae said, her voice gentler than usual.

I finally took in the room I was in. It was an infirmary, much like the one in DuMoir Castle, but this one was a little bit different. I was sure I was still at the Silver Moon Academy.

Shane had come all the way here? Of course he had. He stared at me with pure concern in his dark eyes. I squeezed his hand. "I'm fine." They probably had given me more elixir and done whatever they had to neutralize the dragon's magic. "I'm sorry you had to come all the way here."

"As if I wouldn't have come." He straightened his shoulders. "Besides, Thea said she had something to tell us."

"Oh?" I turned to Thea.

"Yes, I was waiting for you to wake up." She averted her eyes and pressed her lips tight.

Almae stepped to her side and placed a hand on her shoulder. "While you were out, we did another examination on you."

This didn't sound too good. "All right. And?"

She glanced from me to Shane, then back to me, her eyes growing more sorrowful. "I'm so sorry to tell you this, but Raika ... you're dying."

6

SHANE

THE MOMENT DRAKE CALLED ME SAYING WE SHOULD GO TO THE Silver Moon Academy, I knew something serious was going on. When I arrived, I advanced on Raika, growling at Thea and Almae, who hovered over Raika as if she was a precious jewel. She was my precious jewel. They told me to calm down or they would spell me away from the room.

I growled again, but backed away. I asked Lavinia what was going on.

"I don't know," she said. "They are talking in hushed tones, even I can't hear it." And Lavinia was a freaking vampire.

After a few minutes, Thea and Almae told me to sit down and wait. They would talk to us once Raika was awake. That, though, took hours. As the clock ticked by, I grew anxious and demanded they either woke up Raika, or told me what the hell was the problem? Because there was a problem, wasn't it? Why all the secrecy then? But again, they threatened to take me out of the room by force if I didn't behave. Another growl rose through my throat, and my instinct was to tell them "I would like to see you try." But these were two of the most powerful witches in existence. If they wanted me out of here, there wasn't much I could do. So I stayed seated beside Raika, holding her hot hand.

When Raika woke up, I braced myself.

Almae said, "I'm so sorry to tell you this, but Raika ... you're dying."

I had been expecting bad news.

But not this bad.

Everyone around us went quiet. Raika turned big, blue eyes to me.

I blinked. This was a joke, right? A bad one. "I'm sorry, I heard you wrong." A chuckle escaped my lips. "I thought you said—" I swallowed hard, my throat dry. The sympathy and sorrow on Thea's and Almae's faces told me they weren't joking.

Baring my teeth, I shot to my feet and snarled. The chair fell back behind me, echoing through the silent room. Raika flinched.

"Shane, calm down," Killian called. "Being mad won't—"

I turned to him and snarled some more. By now I was sure my eyes shone bright and a little fur covered my arms.

"Shane." A whisper.

My arms drooped by my side.

Slowly, I faced Raika. In this moment, she looked small, fragile, and my instinct was to wrap her in bubble wrap and not let her take one step without checking if it was safe first.

She rested a hand on my arm and offered me a soft smile, unshed tears in her eyes. "Calm down," she said, her voice thin. "Please."

My will was to fight. Who, what? I didn't know. I just wanted to hit something hard right now. But when Raika slid her hand into mine and tugged me closer, I fought to rein in my rage and frustration. They were contained by a thin, frail wall of desperate will, but for a little while, I might be able to stay quiet.

I held her hand tighter in mine and stepped closer to her, standing by her side.

She turned her eyes to the witches. "You said I'm dying," her voice broke, "as if there's nothing we can do."

"We don't know," Thea said. For the first time since meeting the Silverblood queen months ago, I saw her falter. This was painful for her too. "We always knew the dragon's magic might be too much for a human, though when we examined you yesterday, the magic seemed to be merging with you and your darkfire, adapting to you. We were hopeful that you were somehow strong enough to hold it. But when we examined you just now, we saw that the dragon's magic is indeed merging with you, but in doing so, it's sapping your energy. It's taking over your organs and muscles and everything else."

Raika frowned. "I don't feel anything."

"Think of it like cancer," Almae said. "Sometimes they go for years with a cancer festering inside them, until one day, they faint or have a terrible pain, and find out the cancer is already too advanced for treatment."

Thea nodded. "For now, you won't feel more than what you're feeling now. Just an immense power inside you, a little unstable and hard to control. Sometimes you'll feel tired, but it's just a matter of time before that changes."

I clenched my fists. "How long?" Thea turned her gray eyes to me. "How long until that happens? How long until —?" I clamped my mouth, unable to say it. In a way, I still thought this was all a nightmare.

"Until I die," Raika finished for me.

My gut twisted. My grip on her hand tightened.

"We don't know," Almae said. "We don't have experience with this."

Something sparked inside of me. "Then that means this isn't final." I held on to that with both hands. "There might be a cure, some way of treating her." I grabbed my phone from my back pocket. "I can call Kaz. He might know something."

"I can call Evelyn," Lavinia said. I met her eyes, glad someone was on my side and not giving up. "There are also plenty of books here, in DuMoir Castle, and the Silverblood Estate."

"We can contact all of your friends," I added, now on a roll. "Everyone here knows at least another powerful supernatural with great knowledge. Someone has to know something, or at least have an idea about how we can undo this."

Thea and Almae exchanged a look. Thea glanced at Drake. He gave her a slight nod.

Thea sighed. "Of course, we can try everything we can, if Raika agrees to it."

Everyone looked at Raika. She sat on the bed, her face pale, her blue eyes huge and glowing from unshed tears. "Hm." She moved her mouth. Her brows curled down. "Sure. We can try whatever you think might work."

I frowned, not liking the wavering of her voice.

"But Shane," Almae started. "We'll do everything we can to save Raika, but we're treading in unknown waters here. I want you to prepare yourself." She shifted her eyes to Raika. "You too, dear."

Raika nodded.

I didn't care what they thought. We were finding a damn cure, even if I had to sell my soul for it.

"I'm sorry," Thea muttered, the sadness clear in her tone.

"I'm sure you two have lots to discuss." Almae shooed the others toward the door. "We'll leave you two alone for a little while. Call us if you need anything."

Lavinia didn't want to leave, but Killian put an arm around her shoulder and guided her out of the room. Everyone walked out as if they had lost already.

I couldn't allow that.

The door closed behind them with a definitive click.

I let go of Raika's hand and started pacing beside the bed. I had to make a list. Contact Kaz, contact Evelyn, stop by the library in the academy—

"Shane."

Make a pile of all the books about magic, spells, dragons, dragon shifters and—

"Shane."

Do the same at the Silverblood Estate and DuMoir Castle. Go through all the books. Bookmark the pages wherever there was something that looked promising—

"Please."

Her voice broke and that broke me.

I froze, my back to her. My chest hurt and something stung behind my eyes.

This couldn't be happening.

Inhaling deeply, I turned to her. Her eyes reflected mine—pure agony and tears brimming in them.

She extended her hand to me and at that moment I felt like a jerk. Here I was, raging about my own feelings when she was hurting as much, if not more than me.

I stepped to her side and took her hand in mine. "You'll be fine. You have to be fine. We'll find a cure, a spell, something to fix this, and—"

"Shane," she whispered. "I appreciate that, and I'll do what I can too, but Almae is right. There's no guarantees. You should prepare." A sob racked her chest. "By the moon, we have to tell Minsi and Tyren. Prepare them too."

I shook my head. "No. We don't need to fucking prepare. You're not going anywhere."

She offered me a sad smile and a tear rolled down her cheek. "I don't think Thea and Almae would joke about this. If they said my chances are minimal, we should believe them."

"They never said that."

"It was implied."

"Raika, I can't." I brought our joined hands up to my mouth, pressed a kiss to the top of hers. "I know I keep repeating this, but I lost you twice already. I won't survive a third time. I don't want to."

"You have to. For Minsi and Tyren, and the pack."

"I don't care about the pack!" I almost shouted.

"Then think about your brother and sister. They need you. They will need you for a long time. You need to be strong and hang on and stay here for them."

I leaned forward, resting my forehead on hers. Her skin was hot, hotter than it had been yesterday. "I can't lose you."

"You won't." Another tear rolled down. I reached up, cupped her beautiful face, and wiped the tear away with my thumb. I always be with you, even after I'm gone."

"Don't say that," I snarled.

I pulled back, afraid to kiss her or touch her and ignite the dragon's magic again. But I couldn't let go of her completely, so I held her hand in both of mine.

"I'm fine now." She wiped another tear before it fell. "Let's enjoy the moments we have together."

Easier said than done. I wouldn't accept this. Fate hadn't made me want her for all of my life just to take her from me like this. We had to have a happily ever after. I would make sure of it.

My breath caught. "I promise you, I'll find a way to save you."

"You can't promise that."

"Yes, I can. I will find a way," I repeated, hoping the moon heard me and sent me a solution.

But even without the moon, I wouldn't give up.

I wasn't going to lose Raika.

7

SHANE

THAT EVENING, WE WENT BACK TO DUMOIR CASTLE. AS SOON as we arrived, Thea asked Almae, Elisa, and Lavinia to help her prepare a suite close to the infirmary for Raika and me. They drew a witch's circle around the room, spelled its walls so if Raika lost control, she didn't burn down the castle.

Meanwhile, I took Raika to the kitchen to meet the cook: a vampire who had been a baker when human. His name was Morris, he was French, and he had been sixty-two when the previous lord of the castle, Lord Reynard, had found him about to die and turned him.

He was a grump, and often in a bad mood.

"I just wanted to meet the incredible chef behind such amazing food," she told him.

Of course, the old vampire fell head over heels for her. He even smiled at her. "What would you like me to bake for you, ma chérie?"

Raika told him she wasn't hungry, but for tomorrow, she would love freshly baked bread and a mix of oil and herbs to dip the bread in. He got on that instantly. He promised that she would have them for lunch tomorrow along with a whole feast.

"That sounds wonderful," Raika said in her sweet voice, and Morris visibly melted some more.

I almost got jealous. So much, I had to suppress a snarl.

When Raika's suite was ready, the witches called on us.

It was a normal suite, almost like my previous one in this castle—except for the white witch's circle drawn on the floor. Even the bed had been pulled away from the wall a little, so it remained inside the circle.

Once we were settled in the suite, I called Rue and Face-timed with Minsi and Tyren. Of course, they had heard something was going on, but I assured them it was nothing. Raika was still sick and we were treating her.

"Everything is okay," I said, hating I was lying to their faces. "Raika just needs more rest."

After the call, I snuggled with Raika in bed, careful where and how I touched her.

"You should sleep outside the circle," she said.

I shook my head and held tighter to her. "I'm not leaving you."

She smiled and settled even closer to me.

Then we slept.

I COULDN'T SLEEP. I TOSSED AND TURNED, BUT I KNEW I WAS bothering Raika, so I moved to the couch in the suite's seating area. For a couple of hours, I was able to rest my eyes, but the couch was too small for me, and my head spun with a million thoughts, and my veins were filled with worry.

Giving up sleep, I headed to the library at five in the

morning. I had lived in this castle for six months, and I could count on the fingers of one hand how many times I had been inside this library. There hadn't been any reason for me to come in here, especially because every time I walked past it, I remembered Raika and how much she loved books. At the time, I thought she was gone.

Now, that threat was hanging over our heads.

The library was quiet and dark. I turned on a few lights as I walked through the impressive place—the ceiling was at least twenty-five feet high, and tall shelves covered the walls and space in between. The front of the library, and the back where the windows were located, were filled with long wooden tables with small lamps and several cushioned chairs.

For the good part of an hour, I strolled around the shelves, pulling all the books I could find about spells, unwanted magic, dragons, and dragon shifters.

I took them all to one of the long tables and divided them by subject. I was determined not to leave this place until I found something promising, even if it was the first spark of an idea. However, I still hoped we would open one of these books and find the exact answer to what we were looking for.

My research didn't start off well. Skimming through a book about dragons and dragon shifters, I found an entire, albeit short, chapter about humans who had attempted to become dragon shifters. The dragon had to willingly give the human at least half of his magic and perform a ritual in order to create a dragon shifter. If the magic was stolen, and if the dragon didn't perform the ritual, the human died. As far as the book's author knew, no other dragon shifter had been bestowed the gift directly from a dragon. Alice had been the only one, and the other dragon shifters were her descendants. However, according to the author, nothing about dragons and dragon shifters was confirmed. His writings were speculation since no one had seen either species in many centuries.

I fished my phone out and checked the text app. On the way back to DuMoir Castle last evening, I had called Kaz, but he hadn't answered. I left him a couple of texts, but so far I had no replies.

I had also called Evelyn, even though Lavinia said she would contact her. Evelyn didn't answer, but she did send me a text saying she was busy and would call me later. I almost texted back saying it was an emergency, but gave up.

I rested my phone on the table and continued my research. The pile of useless books was growing high, fast.

"There you are."

I lifted my head. Raika entered the library. She wore a different pair of ripped jeans and a tank top, and her hair was damp.

"What time is it?"

"Nine."

Shit, I had been at this for four hours and I had barely made a dent in all the books in front of me.

I forgot all about the books when Raika smiled and walked toward me.

Completely ensnared in her web, I stood. When she got within arm's length, I grabbed her wrists and pulled her to me. I started leaning over her, then stopped.

"When was the last time you drank the elixir?"

She grabbed my shirt with both hands. "A few minutes ago."

"Good," I growled. I closed my mouth around hers, kissing her softly. All I wanted was to take her deeper into this library, push her against a shelf, and have her right here ... but I couldn't. It hurt me, but I broke the kiss before my lust got the best of me. "Slept well?"

Her brows slammed down. "No. I'm guessing you didn't either."

Holding her hand, I sat down again. She took the chair beside mine. "No. I barely slept all night. So I decided to do something useful."

"You should have woke me." Raika picked up one of the books from the separate piles. "I would have come with you."

"You need to rest."

"So do you." Her blue eyes darkened. "I might be dying, Shane, but I won't keel over at this very second. I'm fine."

For now. The unsaid words hung in the air like a dark cloud bringing a storm.

"I don't want to talk about it."

She turned to me, her knees brushing my leg. "We should. This problem won't go away. If we talk, at least we'll have a plan."

"My plan is to find a cure," I said, my voice tight.

"Shane." She rested her hand on my arm and I yanked it back. She stared at me with wide eyes.

"Sorry." What the hell was I doing? I hung my head low, ashamed of myself. "I think I'm losing it."

She slid her fingers through my hair and tilted my head, and I twisted my torso, so my forehead pressed to her shoulder. "I know what you mean. If I stop to think about it, I'll go insane too. I'm not afraid of dying, but I'm afraid for you, for Minsi and Tyren. I want to make sure you three are taken care of before ..." She took a long breath in. "I can't let my emotions win, otherwise I'll spend the rest of my days crying in bed."

I moved my head and rubbed my nose on the soft spot between her shoulder and neck. I didn't want to move from this place ever again. "Maybe we should. Lie down in bed, snuggle, and forget about the world."

"We can't."

I lifted my head and reached for a book. "We need to research."

She touched my hand. "That's not the only reason." My gut tightened. The way she said it. What was it now? "I need train so I can take on Paimon."

I stared at her. "Didn't you hear Thea and Almae yesterday? There will be days you'll be too weak to move. What if you confront him and faint?"

"Hopefully, that won't happen. The witches can make me an elixir to drink that will give me more energy. Before that, we'll deal with those days when they come. But between them, I want to keep training."

I shook my head. "I understood when you first wanted to fight Paimon. I get it. You're the only one who can. But that was before we learned what's happening to you. I don't want you to spend the rest of your days training and then fighting. That will take too much of you and speed up this whole fucking thing!" My anger was rising again.

"I can't live a fairy tale while the rest of the world burns." Her voice rose too. I rarely saw Raika like this.

"It isn't about fairy tales; it's about spending time with your family and finding a cure."

She slapped her hand on a book. "Shane, I will be forever grateful if you find a cure, but I doubt you will. No one has experience with this kind of magic, and time is flying. You should work on accepting what is happening, and if by some miracle I live, then we celebrate. But from now on, I'll be acting as if I'm dying in a couple of weeks. I want to fight and leave this Earth knowing I did all I could to make it a better place for you and your siblings."

My throat closed. My eyes stung. I couldn't breathe.

I shook my head. No, no. Raika wasn't dying. I refused to accept that. I wouldn't, not until the last second. She wanted to fight. Fine, I couldn't stop her, but then neither would I. I would search every crook and corner of this world until I found a way of curing her.

"Fine," I snapped. "Go ahead. Kill yourself faster."

Her shoulders sagged. "Shane ..."

I flipped the page of the book in front of me, but I couldn't see any of the words.

Footsteps reached my ears and I looked up.

Minsi, Tyren, and Rue walked in the library.

Shit. Had they heard anything?

8

RAIKA

I PERKED UP WHEN I SAW MINSI, TYREN, AND RUE WALKING into the library. I wouldn't let my grim fate keep me from having a great time with them.

I pushed from the chair and walked to them. "Good morning."

Minsi ran to me and wrapped her arms around my waist. Tyren glanced from Shane to me, to the books on the table. "What's going on?"

"Nothing," I said quickly. "Your brother is researching something."

"About your sickness?"

"Something like that."

"What is it?" he asked, more closed off than usual. "What do you have?"

"Uh, we don't know exactly." I gestured to the books. "Thus the research." I put a hand on his shoulder and turned him away. "But you know what? We should go some-where else. How about the back garden beside the maze? There are plenty of benches and shade there, and I could ask for food." I pressed a hand to my stomach. "I haven't eaten yet."

I didn't look back as we walked out of the library and went in the direction of one of the back doors that led to the gardens. I didn't know much of the castle yet, but that I could find.

As we walked, I glanced at my phone. I had to be mindful of the time. I was allowing myself only one hour after drinking the elixir to be out and about. After that, I had to stay in my suite until the next dose. This way, the chance of me bursting into flames near others was small.

Outside, the warmth of the day greeted us and I tilted my chin to take in the sunlight and the soft breeze. We found a stone bench under a thin tree, with a good amount of shade.

"I'm so glad you guys came to visit me," I said as I sat down. Minsi sat on my lap, Rue took a place beside me, and Tyren stayed on his feet, looking to this side and the other, as if searching for danger.

"Someone missed you." Rue bopped Minsi's nose. She looked at me, her old eyes knowing. "How are you?"

I forced a smile. I knew she understood everything behind it. I had thought so much about preparing the kids, but now I couldn't even imagine myself telling them about what was happening. I would, though. Soon. But first, whenever I could, I would pull Rue aside and tell her. She would help me break the news to Minsi and Tyren when the time came.

"I'm okay," I said. "I'm happy you all are here. Did you have breakfast already?"

Minsi nodded.

"Well, I haven't. How about we invite some of our friends and have a picnic brunch outside?"

Minsi's eyes rounded, in eagerness.

"I think that's a marvelous idea," Rue said.

"Can I text Hugh so he can come?" Tyren asked.

"Of course. Tell him to invite Lucille too." I picked up my phone and texted Lavinia, Thea, and Almae. They answered right away. Lavinia promised to arrange for the food, Almae said she would help her, and Thea would bring Aurora out.

We were going to have one great day outside.

A few minutes later, Aurora ran from the back door, her dark curls bouncing. When Minsi saw her, she perked up.

"Want to play?" Aurora asked, offering her hand to Minsi.

Minsi nodded, taking the younger girl's hand. They ran toward the rosebushes a few feet to the side and I smiled. Finally, Minsi had a friend.

"They seem to like each other," Thea said from behind us. She had a basket in one arm and red and white checkered fabric folded over the other. "I heard someone wanted a picnic."

I helped her open the big picnic blanket on the lawn, and we opened the basket, which was full of plates, utensils, glasses, and napkins.

We sat down on the blanket and watched as Aurora spelled the roses to dance while they ran around them.

"She's so powerful," I said, watching the girls.

Thea nodded. "Sometimes I worry that her powers are too much for her." Her words had an echo of sorrow to them. She frowned. "How are you?"

I looked around. Tyren was a few feet away, along the path that led to the maze, messing with his phone, and the girls were entertained. Hopefully, no one would listen to me.

"Right now, I'm fine, but I can feel the dragon's magic moving inside me. I think, if we're going to stay out here for a while, I might need to drink elixir sooner. Just this time. After this, I promise to confine myself to my room."

"Why confine yourself?" Rue asked.

I took a deep breath and told her the truth. Her eyes misted as my story went on.

"Right now, I'm worried about the kids," I confessed. "Minsi more than Tyren. Shane told me how hard it was for her when they thought I was dead, how she had frequent panic attacks and it was hard to deal with."

Rue nodded. "I learned most of the techniques you used with her, I tried them, and it worked to some degree, but it was not the same. I'm not you. No one is."

"That's what I'm afraid of." Having me die for a second time might break her. Or she would be hanging on to the idea that I would come back somehow, and she would go crazy that way.

"I can talk to Almae and Lavinia," Thea said. "I'm sure we can make a mild elixir that will calm her down a little, just enough to bring her back when she's losing herself to a full panic attack."

"That would be great," I said with a small smile. "Thank you."

Aurora disappeared inside the castle with her vampire speed.

"What happened?" Thea asked, glancing from Minsi to the castle.

Minsi shrugged.

A few seconds later, Aurora ran back out and halted right in front of Thea and me. She offered me a stuffed yellow bunny. "Here."

I frowned. "That's a pretty bunny."

She kept holding it. "It's for Minsi."

Slowly, I took the bunny from her. "Oh, that's nice of you, but—"

"It's enchanted," the girl said. "I just spelled it. Whenever Minsi starts panicking, ask the others to give her the bunny. It'll calm her down."

I stared at Aurora, amazed. I had heard so much about this half-witch, half-vampire who was supposed to be the next Queen of All Witches, but words didn't do justice to how it was to be in her presence and talk to her, and interact with her. She was seven, but there were times that she behaved like she was seventeen. Hell, like she was twenty-seven! She spoke in such a wise, no nonsense manner, and the look in her eyes seemed so experienced and unflinching.

"Thank you," I whispered as tears sprouted to my eyes.

Then she turned around and skipped toward Minsi, who was still running around the dancing roses.

I turned to Thea, my eyes wide.

She shrugged. "Don't look at me. She's my child, I have rarely been away from her, and she still finds ways to amaze me."

"She heard us and then she brought me a solution." I placed the bunny on my lap. "Amazing."

"I worry about her, though," Thea said, surprising me. "With her being who she is, the future Queen of All Witches, I can only wonder what kind of great destiny she'll have. We already seem involved in some conflict or other every few months. How will it be when she's older?"

I shook my head, unable to imagine it. How would I handle having a seven-year-old with so much promise ahead of her? I would probably hide her from the world. "That must be hard."

"And now there are the night terrors," Thea said.

"Shane told me about that."

"It doesn't happen often, but when it does, the entire castle shakes. It's insane. Every time, we evacuate everyone, afraid the castle will come down." Wow, the chaos that might be. "We've tried spells, elixirs, meditation ... nothing works."

I reached over to her and squeezed my hand. "I don't know what to say other than you and Drake are amazing parents, and if someone can figure this out, that someone is you. You've got this."

Thea offered me a sad smile. "Thanks."

A giggle came from the rosebushes and I was delighted to see that it came from both girls. Aurora was back to behaving like a happy seven-year-old girl, and Minsi, despite being older, was having a great time too.

Seeing her like this warmed my heart.

Footsteps came from the side of the garden. Lucille and Hugh walked toward us.

"I heard you guys are having a party," she said.

Hugh waved at us, but turned toward Tyren. Knowing the two of them, they would spend the entire time hovering close by, but not close enough, on phones either playing games or on social media.

"Not a party, but a get-together." I patted the blanket and she sat down beside me.

She looked at me. "I heard you're sick."

I waved her off. "No talk about anything depressing like that. I forbid it. We're here to have a good time."

"A good time, you say?" Lavinia asked. I glanced toward her voice. She, Almae, and Chef Morris walked out of the castle, carrying large trays. They set the trays right in the center of the blanket.

Chef Morris picked up a plate from one of the trays and

offered it to me. "Just as you asked, ma chérie." It was the warm bread with the herbs and oil dip.

My mouth hanging open, I took the plate. "This is amazing. Thank you so much."

"Anytime, ma chérie." He smiled at me, bowed his head slightly, did the same to Thea, and returned to the castle.

"Is he always like this?" I put the bunny aside before I got it dirty, and set the plate on my legs.

"Morris? Never!" Thea shook her head. "He practically doesn't leave the kitchen, much less talk to anyone."

I smiled, happy for this small thing. I ate a piece of the bread dipped in the oil and almost moaned. I put the plate in the middle along with the other delicious food—pastries and finger foods I had never seen before—so everyone could have a little.

I looked around. Lucille, Lavinia, Thea, Almae, Minsi, Aurora, Tyren, Hugh. They all seemed content in this little improvised picnic, and that made me happy. We were missing our men or this little party would be even more perfect.

It saddened me that Shane was handling this situation worse than I was, but If the situation was reversed, I would probably lose it too. I just hoped he came around before it was too late.

For now, I enjoyed the company of friends, old and new, and family. Knowing Minsi and Tyren had so many people who would watch over them after I was gone was a big relief.

After this little respite, I could focus on training and defeating Paimon without distractions or worries.

9

SHANE

RAIKA'S ENTIRE BEING CHANGED WHEN MINSI, TYREN, AND RUE showed up. That had been a surprise, but maybe a good one. Wasn't I saying Raika had to spend more time with her family?

There you go.

She left with them without looking at me. All of them acted as if I hadn't been here. That wasn't a bad thing. With my temper, I would snap at them if they even glanced my way.

I looked back at the book in front of me. The words were a blur and I couldn't make sense of any of it.

I pushed the books away and leaned back in the chair, my neck resting on top of the backrest. Why was this happening? Hadn't we suffered enough? We had lost almost everyone, lost our town, our pack lands, and now we had to lose Raika too?

A pain cut through my chest, so deep, so raw, it took my breath away.

If she died, I wouldn't survive it. Not this time. I knew

Minsi and Tyren needed me. The pack too. I just ... didn't care anymore.

In need of occupying my mind and moving my body, I decided to go on with my day as normal. Like Raika said, she wouldn't keel over right now, and my feelings and thoughts on the subject were still too messy for me to analyze them.

As I walked to the village, I couldn't ignore the beautiful July day. The sun shone high, the temperature wasn't too hot, the trees and shrubs along the path were still green and abundant. The flowers' sweet scent filled the air. Birds flew overhead. A perfect day, as if mocking my mood.

I went first to my house in the village where I ate some breakfast, took a shower, and changed my clothes. Then, as I walked to the town hall, I texted Dom and Killian to meet and discuss pack business.

Next, I called Kaz.

Again, the phone went directly to voicemail. I texted him, but by now I was wondering if he had ditched his phone before going wherever the dragons were hiding.

I entered my office, sat on the chair behind my desk, and called Evelyn.

"Hey," she answered. "Sorry I've been so hard to find. Ash and I are in rural Mexico and the cell reception here sucks."

"Rural Mexico? What the hell are you doing there?"

"Following traces of dragon magic, what else?"

Right, I knew that.

"So," she went on. "How's Raika?"

I let out a long breath and told her the grim news. "I know you said you would research dragon magic in humans, but now I was wondering if you could research how to save her."

Evelyn didn't answer right away. "I'm sorry, Shane. Saving Raika is more important than what we are doing right now.

I'll go back to Mexico City. I heard there's a light witch coven there. I can contact them and ask if they know anything. If they don't, I can ask to use their library. I'm sure they would be okay with that."

"Thanks, Evelyn."

"Of course, Shane. Anything for you." She paused. "We'll find something. We'll save her."

My throat closed and I blinked fast. "I believe you."

We disconnected and I took a long breath, trying to calm myself. I was here to deal with the pack's problems, not to cry over Raika and her fate.

I pulled out the latest ledger where we kept the pack's records and skimmed it. Dom and I hadn't written on it in a long time. There was still a lot to cover from the year the pack had been enslaved by Conri. With Raika's help, I had noted key dates. According to her, all the days were the same. There wasn't much to report. But I wanted to be as throughout as we could.

In the older records, some important information was missing, like the crystals, the dragon ... things that had only been told from alpha to alpha. My father had died before I had learned it all, and I didn't want to make the same mistake with Tyren, or my childr—

The sudden realization that I would never have children, and one of them wouldn't be alpha, took my breath away and brought another pang of pure pain across my chest.

Raika would die before we got married and had kids.

I rubbed my chest. This hurt more than I thought it could.

"Hey, man, what's wrong?" Dom entered the office. I had been so distraught, I hadn't even heard him approaching. He rounded the desk and pressed a hand to my back. "Shane, you're scaring me."

I took a deep breath and waved him away. "I'm fine." I shook my head. "I take that back. I'm not fine."

He retreated a step and looked at me. "What is it?"

"Remember Raika is sick?"

He nodded.

"It's worse than that. She's dying."

He froze. I told him all we knew so far. Killian arrived in the middle of my tale, but remained quiet as a statue along the wall beside the door, listening. He knew all of this already.

"Shit, man, I'm sorry." Dom shook his head. "I'm sure that with everyone working together, we'll find a solution. Let me know if you want help with your research. Things have been slow over here."

"I appreciate that." I rolled my shoulders and changed gears. "All right, but I didn't ask you two here to talk about that. I want to talk about a second beta and new council members. And also about Tyren."

"Tyren?" Killian frowned. "What did he do?"

"Nothing, but I realized that if Raika dies—" My voice broke. I cleared my throat. "I won't have any heirs. I know Tyren is young, but he's the next alpha. We need to start training him for real and tell him everything we know. He should even start participating in these meetings."

"Does he know about Raika?" Dom asked.

"Raika said we had to prepare the kids, but knowing her, she lost the nerve and hasn't told them yet. But she will, and when she does, we take Tyren on. He'll be my second beta until he becomes alpha."

Dom and Killian nodded.

"What about the council members?" Killian asked.

"We need more, and I've been thinking about a few

names. Lydia, for one, and Jones." Both older wolves who had been in the pack for a long time. "And maybe Lucille. It might be good to have another younger perspective in the group. Any objections?" Both of them shook their heads. "Good, then that's settled. Moving on to—"

"Actually, I have news," Killian said, his tone grim.

Oh, this couldn't be good. "What?"

"I was with Lord Drake this morning when a report came from the demon hunters. Apparently, Paimon found a mage. From what we know, he was the only one who had a key that opened a portal to another realm."

I shook my head. "Wait ... a mage? Portal? Another realm?" I had heard of portals and different realms before, but mages? That was new.

"What realm?" Dom asked.

"We don't know for sure," Killian said. "There are an infinite number of realms. No one knows them all."

My brow furrowed. "So he went to this supernatural to get the key to the portal. This can't be good."

"Has he done anything with it?" Dom asked.

"We don't know," Killian said. "The demon hunters are trying to find out more, but right now they believe Paimon is using this realm to hide."

"Is this key like the fae medallion that can open a portal anywhere, or like the underworld gates, in specific places?" I asked.

"We don't know." Killian seemed as frustrated as I was. "Like I said, the demon hunters are doing all they can to find out that too. I'm sure they will share the information with us once they have it."

"But if Paimon is hiding in another realm, then they will

never find him. He'll find us. He'll open a portal right on top of our heads and attack when we least expect it."

Killian nodded. "That's exactly what Drake said."

This new development was worrisome. We needed to talk to the demon hunters, figure out more about this mage and this portal. We had to know where it went to. Someone had to know something. Hopefully, there was another one of these keys and we could get a hold of it.

Killian's phone rang. He glanced at the screen and frowned. "It's Drake," he said. "Yes?" he answered.

"Bring Shane," Drake said. "We're meeting in ten minutes."

10

RAIKA

I HAD A WONDERFUL TIME WITH MY FAMILY AND FRIENDS. MINSI played like never before and Aurora treated her kindly. Tyren and Hugh remained a little reclusive, most of the time on their phone, but whenever a female vampire walked by, they stared at her. A few weeks ago, Tyren had been so into Lucille, but that seemed to have passed.

Rue was emotional, but she held it together. I made sure to tell her she meant a lot to me and that I appreciated everything she had done for me and for the kids. And now I would need more from her.

"Don't be silly," she said, tears in her eyes. "I do it because I love them."

Lucille caught on that something was wrong, but I didn't want to spoil my mood, so I told her to ask Rue later.

Thea enjoyed watching, and Lavinia and Almae teased each other. The aunt and niece duo had only met seven months ago, and they had been spending a lot of time together.

Two hours into our picnic, dragon's magic grew restless. I

told them all to continue the picnic for as long as they wanted, but I was done. I needed to drink the elixir and stay in my suite.

I entered the castle and a sense of loneliness fell over me. I left them all behind, including Shane. I would leave them all behind forever. What I had told Shane earlier was true. I wasn't afraid of dying, but I was afraid of not being here when Minsi had a panic attack, when she had a terrible nightmare and needed someone to hug her, when Tyren and Shane fought and someone needed to intervene, when he found his mate and wanted to celebrate, when they got married.

Leaving Shane with a broken heart.

That was what hurt the most.

The emotions swirled inside of me, agitating the dragon's magic. My hands shook as I entered my suite, found the elixir, and drank it. I sat on my bed, taking several lungfuls of air, my mind blank. Slowly, the elixir acted and my hands stopped shaking.

A knock came at the door.

My heart kicked up a notch and I stood, apprehensive.

Thea opened the door and walked in. My shoulders deflated. "You were expecting someone else."

I shrugged. "He probably wouldn't knock."

She nodded. "Whatever it is, don't worry, he'll come around."

I knew he would. He was my fated mate. We loved each other fiercely. "We're wasting time."

She stared at me, her gray eyes so serious. "Before, you were determined to control the dragon magic and help us fight Paimon. If you've changed your mind, I understand. We won't pressure you into doing anything you don't want to."

I shook my head. "I haven't changed my mind. I still want to fight him."

She pressed a hand over her chest. "That's good to hear. Then, if you're ready, let's go train."

———

THEA DIDN'T WANT TO WASTE TIME SO WE DIDN'T GO TO THE Silver Moon Academy. Instead, we went deep into the woods, to a big clearing.

"What if I lose control and start a huge fire?" I asked, looking around the tall, thick trees forming the clearing's perimeter.

Thea drew a witch's circle with her magic. "This should contain it."

"And if it doesn't?"

She glanced at me. "If it doesn't, then I can stop it."

I looked at her. Thea was twenty-eight, but she had stopped aging when she was twenty and her soul had linked with Drake's. In some ways, she looked younger than me. Her golden hair fell into immaculate waves around her shoulders and her beautiful dark blue gown and her high heel stilettos felt sorely out of place in the middle of the forest. But that didn't seem to faze her one bit. No, it only added to her allure and power.

As for me, I had my usual cropped shorts, tank top, and combat boots. I didn't put fishnet tights on because it was too hot out.

If a stranger walked in on us right now, he would be lost.

I remembered something. "I drank the elixir minutes ago. Shouldn't we wait a couple of hours?"

"Actually, I want to start training with the elixir at its

strongest," Thea said. "Perhaps if you can learn how to control the dragon's magic while its numbed, then you will have a better chance of controlling it when it's at its full force."

It made sense. I rolled my shoulders. "I'm ready."

"Good. Then let's try the same thing from yesterday. Call on your darkfire in one hand, and the dragon magic in the other. Try maintaining both at the same time."

I inhaled and exhaled a couple of times, emptying my mind, calming my soul.

I could do this.

I knew I could do this.

Knowing it would be harder to call the dragon magic while it was numb, I started with it. I found it half-asleep inside me, entwined with my darkfire, around my veins and organs. It was a part of me now, there was no doubt of that.

The magic resisted my call. It dodged my hold, but I wasn't going to let it get away. I dug my heels into the ground, gritted my teeth, clenched my fists, and groaned as I reached for the magic and its stubbornness. Slowly, inch by inch, the magic reluctantly woke up from a nap. It answered, in a clumsy way, and came to the surface.

"The magic will be weaker," Thea said, "but it might also be harder to control. Hang tight to it."

I did. With a groan, I opened my hand and a small flame the size of a golf ball floated in the air above my palm. I wanted to rejoice that I had done it again, but it took my entire concentration to keep it there.

"Now the darkfire," Thea said.

By the moon ...

A little more used to me, the darkfire answered right away, but because most of my focus was on keeping the dragon magic alive, it was still hard, a lot harder than usual, to call on it, bring it to the surface, and hold on to it.

The darkfire sparked to life in my other hand, much bigger and solid than the dragon's magic.

"Good," Thea said. "Now make the dragon's magic bigger. Control it."

Sweat beaded my forehead as I gritted my teeth, braced my core, and held on to the magic running through me, within me, around me. In my mind, I drew a line dividing my being into two. On one side, the bigger one, the darkfire, on the other, smaller side, the dragon's magic. I took in a deep breath and focused on balancing the sides.

The dragon's magic fought me the entire time. It pushed and pulled, like a stubborn child who wanted to be the favorite. There were no favorites! These two damn magics had to live together in peace, at least while I was alive.

A cry ripped from my throat as I pushed the invisible line, trying to make the sides equal in size. The dragon magic in my hand flickered, wavered, but it grew, centimeter by centimeter.

Finally, after what felt like a torturous eternity, the line was right in the middle. The two magics floated above my palms, equal in size. The dragon magic still sparked, as if trying to show me it wouldn't behave so nicely, but for now, it held and didn't push back. I would take this victory.

I exhaled and looked at Thea.

She smiled at me. "Let them go and do it again."

Oh, shit. I knew why. I had to practice calling the magics, do it faster and faster, have the dragon's magic obey me and do what I wanted right from the start ... but I felt like I had finished a marathon, and now I had to do it again.

I dropped my arms, both magic bolts disappearing in the

air, and shook my arms. I took a few seconds to breathe and relax.

And then I did it again.

This time, it was a bit easier, and the dragon's magic was only one-fourth the size of the darkfire.

The next time, it was a little bit easier than the last time, and the dragon's magic was half the size of the darkfire.

The third time, it was easier, and the dragon's magic was three-fourths the size of the darkfire.

It was on the eighth time that the dragon's magic answered almost as fast as the darkfire and it matched the darkfire's size and shape.

By then, I was drenched in sweat, my arms shook with the effort, and a headache had started deep in my temples.

Thea nodded at me, a small smile on her lips. "I know it looks like you're not progressing fast enough, but believe me when I say this, you are. I haven't seen anyone, not even my witches, dominate two warring magics so fast."

I frowned. "Do they have two different magics?"

"Some are half-witches, half ... something else. Warlocks, different kinds of witches, fae ..." She shrugged. "But some-times, for training purposes, we create the illusion that they have two different powers inside them."

"That's cruelty." I was only half joking.

"That's a strong word, but you know by now that our enemies are not kind or considerate. We need to be ready."

I nodded. Yes, I knew that.

She whisked a bottle of water out of nowhere and offered it to me. "Here. Let's have a five-minute break."

Like a lost soul in the desert, I yanked the bottle from her and drank half of it in one go. Tired to my bones, and hot in this warm sun, I sat on the ground, not caring if the grass blades prickled my bare legs.

Thea moved her hands and a cold, gentle breeze blew past me. I inhaled deeply, savoring the moment.

"Thank you."

She sat down in front of me, much more ladylike, with her legs carefully folded under her and hidden by her gown, while I was plopped on the ground, my spine bent, and completely wasted.

"You're doing great."

"Thanks," I said again. I drank the rest of water and wished I had another bottle so I could dump it over my head. Thea worked her magic again and the breeze came back. I could get used to this. "Thank you ... for training me."

Thea shook her head. "You don't need to thank me for that. I like teaching and training, which is one of the reasons I've opened the academy, but you know there's more to this."

"I know. If Paimon wins, then the underworld will go back to the bad side, and who knows what he will do."

"For one, I believe he would call all the demons back to the underworld, which at first would be a good thing. They might stop frightening humans and giving us more work. But I think he wouldn't stop there. Paimon has grown greedy and powerful in the last couple of years. He would gather all demons to attack. He would come for all of us, eventually."

That was certainly not good, and if I could stop it from getting that far, I was all for it.

I pushed to my feet. "Let's continue."

11

RAIKA

THEA AND I TRAINED FOR ANOTHER TWO HOURS STRAIGHT. Despite my exhaustion, I progressed quickly. I was able to conjure both magics instantly, shape them how I wanted, and throw them at the magical targets Thea had spelled.

By now, the elixir was losing its effect, but that was a good thing. As it awoke, the dragon's magic rebelled a little, but because I had trained so much, it was easier to wrangle it into submission.

As the time passed, I grew anxious, though. The longer I stayed without the elixir, the bigger the chance of me blowing up and hurting Thea.

I was about to suggest we stopped for the day when Thea's phone rang. She fished it from a hidden pocket in her gown and smiled at the screen. It could only be Drake.

"Hi," she answered. Her smile faltered and a frown marred her forehead. "All right. We'll be right there." She lowered the phone and said, "We need to go."

I stiffened. "What happened?"

She started walking. "We're being called into a meeting."

I fell into step with her, thinking we were going into DuMoir Castle and probably to Lord Drake's office with some other supernaturals—Shane, Killian, Lavinia, Almae, maybe some of the princes. The usual.

All of these supernatural were in front of the castle. Lavinia saw me coming and walked toward me, the elixir in hand. Thea must have told her to bring it to me, and I was in desperate need of it.

I took it and drank it in one go, doing my best to ignore its foul taste. "Thanks."

"Don't mention it," she said with a small smile.

"What's going on?" I asked, stepping up to the group. Shane was here and though he stood by my side, I could feel the tension rolling from him in waves. Was this because we had parted after a disagreement, or did he know something about this meeting that I didn't?

"He's on his way," Lord Drake said, his tone flat. Whatever was going on was affecting him too.

About ten feet from us, a purple portal appeared. The oval was at least eight feet tall and four feet wide, and a man wearing black leather and a black cloak lined with dark red stepped through it—a warlock.

"Lord Drake." He lowered his head.

"Aspen," Drake said.

Aspen gestured to the portal. "This way, please."

Drake was the first to walk through the portal. Next was Thea. Then the rest of us—Prince Cain, Prince Dorian, Prince Ashton, Killian, Lavinia, Almae, Elisa, Zadkiel, and Dom. Shane and I were the last ones. He offered his hand to me.

I could be a little mad at him, but he was still my mate and the man I loved more than anything. I slipped my hand in his, and he held it tight.

Together, we crossed the portal.

I gasped as I found myself in a known place, but also different. The portal opened at one of the gates to the underworld, where Shane and I had been before. There had been a great number of demon hunters here, but now … now there had to be hundreds of demon hunters, vampires, witches, wolf shifters, and other supernaturals.

We were ushered to a big tent set right beside the gate, where a long table took the center. Norah, Ariella, Prince Gray, and others I did know sat around it.

"Lord Drake, Queen Thea," a young man with brown hair and gray eyes said from the head of the table. He glanced at me. "You must be Raika."

I startled. What? They knew me.

A young woman with long, dark hair sat to his right. Her eyes shone gold. "Hi, Raika. I wish we had met under better circumstances." She stood. "I'm Erin Belmont."

I knew her name. I had heard it before and she had even helped Shane and me before, when we needed to come to the underworld. She had mediated our meeting. She was the famous half-demon hunter and half-demon who took down her father, King Brikan, with her siblings. She was King Tanner's half sister, and princess of the underworld.

"This is Rey Lowe." Erin gestured to the young man beside her. Half-demon, half-human, headmaster of the Blackthorn Hunters Academy, and her partner. Next, she pointed to an older man sitting to Rey's left. "This is Hadrian Walton, the head of the Blackthorn Hunters." The man nodded his head at me. "Is there anyone here you don't know?" She gestured to a few other demon hunters. "These are Ava, Harvey, Doreen, Thierry, Andre, Kaitlin, and Max."

Lord Drake pointed to a few others. "Warlock Lord Keeran, Starlight Alpha Luana, Fae Ambassador Farrah, and Wyatt."

There were too many new faces, too many names, and I had already forgotten half of them.

"Is King Tanner safe?" Drake asked.

Erin nodded. "He's in a special place in the underworld with Princess Jasmin. Only a few of us know where exactly, and how to get in and out."

"Good," Drake whispered.

Rey opened his arms, indicating the chairs around the long table. "Please, sit down."

There weren't enough seats around the table for all of us, but Drake took the other table end with Thea at his right. She patted the spot to her side, and I sat beside her. Shane sat beside me. He and the guy sitting beside him, Wyatt, if I wasn't mistaken, grasped arms in hello. I frowned, realizing Shane probably knew all of these people.

"What is the latest report?" Drake asked, right to the point.

Rey smacked his lips. "We sent a team to check on the mage, and we've confirmed it. Paimon killed him and stole the key to another realm."

I frowned. What? What were they talking about?

"Do you know what realm it is?" Thea asked.

Rey, Erin, and Hadrian shook their heads. "No, we don't," Rey said. "But we think we're running out of time."

"We've increased security at each underworld gate," Erin said. "But if he uses the key and places a portal right in front of a gate, there isn't much we can do."

"So we need to strike him before he uses it," Drake said.

Rey nodded. "The problem now is how to get to him."

Erin rapped her nails on the table. "Right. The problem we're encountering right now is that if Paimon is using this other realm and its portal to move around, then we won't be able to find him. How can we attack a moving target?"

"We've talked about using fae glamour on someone else," Farrah said. She was ridiculously pretty with silver-blond hair and blue eyes. Her pointed ears peeked from underneath her hair, and she looked more like an angel than Ariella did. "One of us pretend to be Tanner and be out in the open, but most of us believe Paimon won't fall for that."

"He's smart," Rey said, and from his tone, it was clear he knew Paimon personally.

Voices rose as the people discussed ideas at the same time. I felt overwhelmed with the amount of powerful supernaturals gathered in one place, and with the amount of information passed around.

"All right, all right," Hadrian called out. In seconds, the tent went quiet. "Here's the one idea I'm hearing the most: leave one gate unguarded. Paimon will know this is a trap, but it'll also be his only chance to get in. He will come. When he does, we strike with all we have."

One third of the supernaturals shook their heads, while the rest nodded.

"Didn't we just say Paimon is smart?" Luana, the Starlight alpha, asked. "He won't fall for it."

"He will because he won't have another chance," a demon hunter said.

"He has the dragon magic now; he doesn't need to wait to come," Ariella said.

"Then what is he waiting for?" another demon hunter asked. "Why hasn't he come yet?"

"Because he only has half of the dragon magic," I said.

"He's strong, a lot stronger than before, but he might not be strong enough to take on a full army by himself."

Hadrian nodded. "That's why, if we create an opening, he'll come."

Again, there were nods and grunts all around the tent.

Rey looked around. "Are there any other viable options?"

No one said a thing.

"Then we do this," Hadrian said. "We need time to prepare, so in two days, we'll retreat from the Florida gate, and hide beyond it. When Paimon shows up, we attack."

"What if he sends his army first?" a warlock asked. I had already forgotten his name.

"We attack," Hadrian said. "We hold the fort and kill as many of them as we can until their spineless leader shows up."

I frowned. Ivy would be with Paimon. He would send her in first. I had to make sure I got to her before the others did.

All eyes fell on me and I went still.

"Raika, will you be ready to take him down?" Rey asked.

My eyes widened. I stared at Thea. She offered me a slight nod.

"Y-yes," I said, aware that I sounded unsure. Beside me, I could swear I heard a faint, short growl.

"We'll keep training nonstop," Thea said, her voice clear, strong.

Rey nodded, his eyes still on me. "I know we're asking a lot from you."

"It's okay." This time, my tone was unwavering. "I'll keep training, and when it's time, I'll be ready." At least, I hoped I would be.

Under the table, Shane held my hand again. I let him entwine his fingers with mine, to give me strength.

"All right." Hadrian shot to his feet. "Let's get the ball rolling. I'll see you all in Florida in two days." He walked away.

The people around the table got up. Some stayed around, talking among themselves, others left the tent and went about their duties.

Shane tugged my hand and I rose with him. Thea turned to me, an encouraging smile on her lips. "Don't worry. I'll help you. You can do this."

She then went to talk to the warlock and the female alpha, who were now holding hands.

I frowned. Shane followed my line of sight. "They are fated mates."

"Oh." That was cool.

"A lot of couples here are." I noticed Shane glancing to Cain, then to Norah. "Even ones that aren't officially a couple."

Erin and Rey walked toward us. I stiffened, but Shane greeted them like old friends.

Erin stepped right into me and wrapped her arms around me. "I know what you're going through." Right. She had had to kill her father. She pulled back and looked at me. "I just wanted to say that you're brave and strong, and I admire what you're doing for us."

"If you need anything for your training, just let us know," Rey told me. "Whatever it is, we'll send it your way."

"Thanks," I muttered.

"Let's go," Drake called from the other side of the tent. "We have much to do."

Shane and I waved at Erin and Rey, at some other supernaturals too, then we followed Drake and Thea out of the tent. Aspen was waiting for us. He opened the portal and we all stepped through. We arrived right where we had left—the front steps of DuMoir Castle.

After thanking the warlock and watching as he left and the portal closed, Lord Drake turned to us. "It's getting late, and we all have much to process. I'll give you all the night off. But tomorrow we'll start early with a meeting." He looked at me. "And with training." I nodded. "Good evening," he said before taking Thea's hand and walking into the castle.

Everyone followed.

And I was suddenly left alone with Shane.

He tugged me closer and I looked at him.

He sighed, his puppy eyes on me. "Can we talk?"

12

SHANE

IT TOOK EVERYTHING IN ME TO REMAIN CALM AND QUIET DURING
the meeting. They all stared at Raika as if she was the ulti-
mate weapon. Maybe she was, but she was *my* mate.

At some point, I had growled, but Drake shot me a death
glare. I knew that if I moved one inch out of line, I would be
kept away from the mission, and that couldn't happen. I had
to be there. I had to be beside Raika the entire time, keeping
her safe.

I was glad that when I took her hand in mine, she didn't
pull back.

We were still holding hands when we crossed back to
DuMoir Castle, and everyone went inside.

I looked at her, my heart tight. "Can we talk?"

She stared at me, her bright blue eyes so poignant. "We
should, yes."

Shit, what did that mean? For a moment, I panicked she
would return her ring to me. That she would tell me she
wasn't going to marry me anymore. If that was the case, I
would take it back. I would never force her to do something

she didn't want, but I sure as hell would do my best to have her accept it again, even if it took a year or a decade.

"Raika, I—"

She tugged my hand. "Let's walk. I don't think I ever walked around the entire castle, seen its full splendor."

I followed her. I would follow her anywhere. Hands linked, we strolled around the castle. The sun was dipping in the horizon, bathing the tall parapets with a golden-orange glow. In the east, the blue sky turned black.

The silence between us was comfortable, but I felt like the words were bubbling in my chest and they would spill over in a messy heap if I didn't say anything.

We turned a corner of the castle, this side already bathed in darkness, and I dropped her hand. I halted, waiting until she turned to me.

"Raika, I'm an idiot," I started. "I have this immense protective feeling inside me. I need to shield you from all the bad things. It's my nature. I'm an alpha! And you're my incredibly beautiful, amazing, strong mate. It's ... hard for me to let go. To give you freedom when I know things won't work out in the end. But I also know I need to. I'm so sorry I freaked out on you earlier. I don't know why I thought you would change your mind about fighting Paimon after—" I clamped my mouth shut, but the emotions were all there, swirling in my chest, pressing against my heart. "After your diagnosis. But I understand why you didn't. I admire your strength and determination. I still would rather keep you inside a protected house where I could keep an eye on you, but I will step back and let you do whatever you need to. I'll be right by your side, supporting you in any way I can."

She took a step closer to me. "There's something I need to do right now."

I frowned. "What is it? Just say it and I'll help you."

She advanced two more steps, rested her hands on my chest, and leaned into me. "You better help me because I'm not doing this alone." She rose onto her tiptoes and lifted her head to mine.

A growl escaped my lips as I met her halfway. I closed my mouth around hers and retreated until her back was against the rough castle stone.

Then I jumped back, my eyes wide. "We can't. You'll lose control and you'll burst into flames again."

She fisted my shirt, tugging me to her. "I drank the elixir not one hour ago. I'm learning to control it. I can keep myself from exploding if we just kiss."

She didn't need to tell me twice. I cupped her face and pressed my mouth to hers again. She parted her lips and I kissed her with all my might. I smoothed my hands down to her waist, conscious of the way her body molded to mine, of the little moan that came from her throat and sent a shot of pure desire across my chest, down to my pants. Raika knotted her legs around my waist and I pressed my hard-on into her hips. Another moan escaped her lips and I almost lost it. My body reacted to hers in the most perfect way.

I needed her. I needed her so much, but I knew I couldn't have her. Not now. Still, it was so fucking hard to back away from her. Her breasts smashed against my chest, her scent filling my nostrils, her delicious taste ... it was impossible.

Her skin warmed up fast.

I broke apart again before it was too late.

Leaned against the wall, Raika frowned and took in deep breaths. She closed her eyes for a moment, probably reaching for her magic and trying to control it.

Then, she opened her eyes. "It's okay." She pushed away

from the wall. "It's under control again. But I should go back to our room and be near the elixir, just in case."

"You should have one on you at all times."

She nodded. "I keep meaning to carry one with me, but I always forget." She started walking to the nearest door.

"Raika," I called.

She skidded to a stop and looked at me.

"We're good, right?"

She smiled at me and extended her hand to me. I walked to her, slipped my hand in hers.

"We are," she whispered. "I love you too much to stay mad at you."

"I love you too." I brought our joined hands up and kissed the top of hers. "Way too much."

Hand in hand, we walked to our suite.

THE NEXT THIRTY-SIX HOURS FLEW BY. RAIKA TRAINED WITH Thea and Almae, and sometimes Lavinia too, nonstop. She had a few short breaks to nap, eat, and shower, but she wanted to keep going while she could.

My protective instinct wanted to step in and growl at everyone for pushing her so hard, but I knew she wanted this. I reined in my frustration and supported her the way she wanted.

I had to say, I was impressed with her progress. She could now summon the darkfire and the dragon's magic without much effort, and fight with both at the same time. I could see how it weighed on her. This new magic was killing her, and I started to think the more she used it, the faster it would happen.

Each time I thought about that, I went for a run. Better to burn my pent-up anger and frustration that way than to argue with her.

When the time came, we all got together at the entrance to DuMoir Castle. Though several of us were going, Lord Drake had ordered full lockdown on the castle and the village, with plenty of vampires serving as guards. He wanted to make sure everyone stayed safe while we were gone.

We teleported to the Florida gate. We arrived in a large clearing and all around us were trees with thick trunks—but two of them were bigger than the others, with their trunks even thicker and reaching higher. Their bark was darker, and their leaves barely moved whenever a breeze blew by.

"That's the gate," Thea said. "It's hidden between the two trees."

I stared at the trees, but didn't see anything. So the gates didn't look all the same? I had not known that.

As planned, we arrived early and met the others inside the portal in the underworld. I couldn't help looking around as we waited. We seemed to be atop a mountain, right beside an endless cliff, but the skies were dark here, and in the distance, all we could see were the thin rivers of lava cutting through the landscape.

It was always tense with so many lords and queens and leaders among us, but Hadrian was in charge now. He divided us in several groups, and sent some of us back through the portal. Because Raika was important for this mission, we were assigned to the same group as Drake, Thea, Erin, Rey, and a bunch of trained demon hunters. Other powerful supernaturals would be close by.

Per Hadrian's instructions, we hid beyond the trees that lined the clearing, and fae and witches created glamours over us. Even if Paimon tried, he wouldn't be able to see or sense us here.

The demon hunters had been spreading rumors that the hunters would be moved and that the gate would be under-guarded for a few minutes. Supposedly, only a few people were knew this, but they made sure more supernaturals were informed.

I still had my doubts that Paimon would show up. I understood Hadrian's logic, but if it was me, would I do it? If my enemy had Raika or Minsi or Tyren, I wouldn't think twice about it. Even knowing it was a trap, I would walk into it.

And Paimon really wanted the underworld.

Raika and I stood with our group among the trees, west of the gate. The glamour over us made us invisible, and it covered most of our scent, but it did little for sounds. So we were all quiet as we waited.

Beside me, Raika's hand shook, and she shifted her weight from side to side. I reached over, grasped her hand, and held it tight. She let out a long breath and rolled her neck and shoulders.

The plan was simple. If Paimon showed up with his demons, most of our fighters would focus on the demons, while a dozen of us went directly for Paimon. We would try to immobilize him while Raika killed him.

I had wanted to kill him myself, but I would be satisfied if Raika did it.

The time passed.

One hour.

Two hours.

We were told to hold on. If Paimon was coming, he could be playing with us, testing our patience.

He was really testing mine.

Three hours.

Four.

Finally, when we had been here for five hours and twenty minutes, sparks shot from the center of the clearing.

A green light appeared, spreading across the portal.

Raika stiffened and I squeezed her hand.

I held my breath, waiting for the demon army to descend upon us.

A minute ticked by. Then another.

We all looked at each other, wondering what to do.

"I'll check it out," Drake said, his voice low.

Thea held his arm, her eyes wide.

The portal trembled and something came through.

I called my wolf, ready to pounce.

Then the portal closed.

What?

We rushed forward. The something that had come through the portal were two people, tangled in a heap. Two demon hunters.

Erin and Rey were the first to reach them. Drake, Thea, Raika, and I were next.

"Oh, no," Raika said, pressing her hand to her mouth.

Rey turned the male demon hunter's body, and laid it on the ground. There was blood everywhere, and his eyes stared up at the sky, unmoving.

The female demon hunter wasn't much better. Erin cradled the hunter's head on her lap and smoothed the blood from her face.

"Talk to me, Letty." Erin's voice broke. "What happened?"

"H-he got us," Letty croaked. "Paimon g-got us when we

were patrolling." She took in a shaky breath. "He wanted us to send you a message."

Erin shook her head. "You don't need to tell me now. We'll get you to a healer, okay?"

"I ... I don't have time," Letty gasped. She clutched Erin's arm. "He said that none of y-you can trick him."

"Thank you for telling me this." Erin gently disentangled Letty's hand from her arm and set her down. "The healer is arriving. Just hang on, okay? Hang on a little—"

Letty's head lolled to the side, and her eyes turned glassy.

Erin inhaled sharply. Raika gasped again. Everyone stood there, watching two dead demon hunters.

Hadrian held his Dawnblade tight and roared, "Paimon, I swear on my life, you'll pay for this!"

13

RAIKA

HADRIAN, ERIN, AND REY BLAMED THEMSELVES FOR WHAT HAD happened, but the only one to blame was Paimon.

We didn't ease up on the portal after Paimon sent the two demon hunters back to us. Drake and Keeran said that the moment we left, Paimon would come. Some suggested we should leave, so he could come. We would turn around and attack. Others said we had enough for the day and called it quits.

A large number of demon hunters, vampires, and witches stayed behind, in case the demon decided to attack. If that happened, we would all jump through a portal and be there a few seconds later to help.

Meanwhile, we were sent back home to rest.

How did we go home and lie in our beds after what happened? Knowing Paimon was out there? Knowing all he had done in the past?

After bidding good night to our friends, Shane and I walked back to the village, hand-in-hand. Since now I had more control over the dragon's magic, I had been allowed to return to the village for short periods of time. Right now, it was to have dinner with our family. And then I was right back at the castle.

I patted the extra elixir in my pocket. I didn't go anywhere without it now.

"Are you okay?" Shane asked, breaking the silence.

I looked up at the blue sky. We still had another hour, maybe one and half hours of sunlight left, and it felt so good to be outside—not too hot, but hot enough to feel the warmth of the sun on my skin.

"I'm feeling terrible for those two demon hunters. Their families. For Erin, Rey, and Hadrian." I sighed. "But otherwise, I'm okay." I leaned my head on his shoulder. "Having a nice meal with our family will cheer me up."

Shane kissed the top of my head. "Let's hope everyone is in a good mood today."

As we walked, my stomach tightened in a million knots. I had to tell Minsi and Tyren about my situation, but honestly, I couldn't bear it. I knew this would cause Minsi to have another breakdown, one that would be close to impossible to come back from. And Tyren ... I had no idea how Tyren would react, I knew it wouldn't be too good.

In the end, when we arrived at the house and were greeted by our family with such love and affection, and everyone was in such a great mood ... I chickened out once more.

At least, we had a great time together.

EARLY THE NEXT DAY, SHANE AND I WALKED FROM OUR SUITE TO the library. He wanted to spend the day researching about how to save me. I appreciated it more than words could say, but I also had a deep feeling that he was wasting time. He had to worry about our pack and their future. I knew he had to do this, so I sat with him behind one of the large tables full of old books while we waited for breakfast. We probably shouldn't eat in the library, but Shane didn't want to waste one minute.

Morris personally brought us the food with a white rose and a special cake. "I made it just for you, ma chérie."

Beside me, Shane growled. I gave him a "really?" look before getting up and embracing the old vampire. "Merci."

Morris pulled back, his eyes filling with tears. "Anything for you."

"Are you okay?" I asked, concerned.

"It's just ... you reminded me of my daughter. She had long, pretty hair like yours, and her eyes were dark green. But your kindness and your contagious smile, they are like hers."

His daughter ... she might have died a long time ago. Poor Morris. "I'm sorry."

He shook his head. "Don't be. Even though she thought I was gone, I made sure she lived a long, happy life. She died of old age and I was right there." He smiled at me. "And now I can look at you and relive those precious moments in my head."

"Then I'm glad." I took a big bite of the cake to please him and it melted in my mouth. "It's divine." It really was.

The old vampire left with a satisfied glint in his eyes.

I put another big bite of cake in my mouth and moaned.

Shane cocked an eyebrow. "I don't know if I should be jealous of the cook or the cake."

I swallowed. "Both, probably."

With a grunt, Shane gave in and took a bit of the cake too. "Shit, okay, it is good." He shoved more in his mouth.

I laughed.

My phone vibrated with a new text.

Thea: *I'm heading out.*

Me: *Be right there.*

Shane swallowed and frowned. "It's time?"

I nodded.

Last evening, after I got back from the village, Thea had asked if I wanted to take a day off, but I told her no.

"Eventually, I'll face Paimon, and when I do, I want to be ready," I had said.

I ate two more bites of the delicious cake, drank half a cup of coffee, and turned to Shane. "I'll see you for lunch, right?"

With a small pout, Shane nodded.

I pressed my lips to his in a quick peck, then stood and walked away before I lost it and melted into him. The last few days had been hard on us. We both wanted to rip our clothes off, but because of this damn dragon's magic, we couldn't.

I prayed to the moon that I gained enough control over it so I could sleep with him one more time before I died. It sounded petty, but honestly, if I had to go, I wanted to go knowing I had enjoyed him thoroughly.

In the corridor outside the library, I saw Lavinia and Elisa, both walking my way.

"Good morning," Elisa said, almost too formal.

"Morning," I said, pausing my steps to talk to them. "Where are you two going?"

"To the library." Lavinia pointed to the doorway a few feet behind me. "We'll help Shane with his research."

"Not just us," Elisa said. "More witches are coming.

Witches here in the castle. The ones at the Silverblood Estate are already at it."

Something burned behind my eyes and I averted my gaze.

Lavinia hooked her arm behind my neck and pulled me to her. "It's okay, Raika. It'll be okay. We'll save you, okay?" She kissed my cheek, then let me go. "Now go train and leave the research to us."

The two of them waved at me and disappeared inside the library. Three other witches turned into the hallway and headed to the library. They too waved at me.

More tears prickled my eyes, and I hurried out of there before I became a blubbering mess.

When I got to the clearing, Thea wasn't alone. Almae was there too.

She smiled at me, like a grandmother would. In this aspect, she reminded me of Rue—a strong presence, always ready to help.

"Ready to train with me, my dear?" she asked, gesturing for me to enter the circle. Almae had participated in my training from the beginning, but she had not been as active as Thea.

"Of course." I halted in the center of the clearing.

"Let's start simple," she said. "With some breathing exercises to clear our minds and activate our magic."

She closed her eyes and took a deep breath. I did the same.

From breathing exercises, we moved on to simple casting —calling both magics, controlling them, shaping them as I wanted, throwing them at targets. Then calling them at different times, switching between them fast, without thinking. Pulling back on one, throwing the other.

Thea cast several blue and silver figures, shaped like humans, and had them blink here and there, and I had to hit them—blue with darkfire, silver with dragon magic. Almost like an advanced whack-a-mole game. It was fun, but tiring, and whenever I made too many mistakes in a short period of time, frustration made me reckless.

Whenever that happened, we took a short break.

We trained for several hours, but when the sun was right above us, making me more tired and hot, Thea called it quits. "Lunchtime. We'll come back in a couple of hours, after everyone has rested, and this sun moves a little."

"You could always create some kind of shield over the clearing," I said, joking.

"I could, or I could have a giant tent installed," she said, matching my tone.

"That too." I walked to her and the three of us entered the forest.

Being among the trees reminded of how we hid yesterday to catch Paimon, and how nervous I had been. If it weren't for Shane by my side, I would have succumbed to fear and had a panic attack myself.

Since then I had been wondering ... "Do you think throwing bolts of magic at Paimon will kill him? Isn't that too little for a demon like him?"

Thea pressed her lips tight. "I have been thinking about that and I'm not sure."

Almae nodded. "I thought about that too. We might need to create a unique spell using your magic for this reason."

I frowned. "But what?"

Almae shrugged. "I don't know."

"We should make a list of ideas," Thea suggested.

I liked that. I made a mental note to get either a notebook or a tablet, and carry it with me wherever I went so I could write down spell ideas. Or I could use my phone. I was sure the first ideas would be silly, but at some point, we would produce something good, right?

We arrived back at the castle. The witches invited me to have lunch with them, but they knew I was going to meet Shane in the library.

As I thought, he had barely moved from his spot behind the long table, only the piles of books had shifted considerably. However, the library was far from quiet and empty right now. As I walked to Shane, who finally lifted his head from the book he was reading, I saw at least a dozen witches working on research.

A small smile spread over my lips. It was good to know no one wanted to see me dead.

I halted in front of Shane, a hand on my waist. "Never thought I would see the day when you spent your entire day reading."

He groaned. "Me neither."

I chuckled as I rounded the desk and got closer to him. "I gotta say, I always loved seeing you among books. Now more than ever."

One corner of his lips tugged up. "Hm, so you like it?" He picked up a book and pretended to read it, focused.

I sat beside him and snatched the book from him. "Now I want you focused on me!"

"Yes, ma'am." He leaned into me and pressed a soft kiss on my lips. "I'm tired of being cooped up here all morning. How about we go outside to eat?"

"I'm tired of being under the hot sun for so long."

He offered his hand to me. "Then let's go to one of the shaded courtyards."

I liked this idea. I slipped my hand into his, and after sending a message to the kitchen about our lunch and where we would be, Shane and I headed to the courtyard.

We had stepped into the beautiful courtyard when his phone rang.

He picked it up and started at the screen. "This can't be good."

"Who is it?"

"Eike." He answered it, "This is Shane."

On the other side of the line, Eike let out a long breath. "I need your help."

A MAID CAME OVER TO TALK TO ME ABOUT LUNCH AND distracted me from Shane's conversation with Eike. He kept walking, pacing in the middle of the courtyard, listening with intent, and that made me worried.

Shane had told me about meeting with Eike when he had visited the Nightshade lands a few weeks ago, when he thought I had died for the second time.

By the time the maid left, Shane turned off the call.

He turned to me, his face somber.

I walked to him. "What happened?"

He blew out a breath. "You remember Eike?"

I nodded. "The Whitecrest wolf who came to you when you were visiting the Nightshade town."

"Yes. He wanted my help then because Jean, Nortrix's son, was too young to rule by himself, and it seemed the pack was divided. He thought a civil war would start."

I held my breath. "And?"

"He was right, but it's much worse than that. Serge killed Jean and became the pack's alpha."

"What?"

"Serge is as bad as Conri was. A rebel group is trying to overthrow him. Eike is with this group, but with Serge's alpha powers, it's difficult."

"I always knew Serge was a prick, but this ... this is too much."

"There's more," Shane said, voice tight. "Delco and the Ironfang are watching the power struggle. Delco came to Eike and offered to help, if the rebels and then the rest of the Whitecrest accept him as the alpha."

"Delco isn't the best choice either."

"I know."

"And he wants you to go there and do what? Kill Serge and become the alpha? Don't we have enough on our hands as it is? I don't want to add a fight with Ironfang to our to-do list."

"He didn't say he wants me to be the alpha, but he wants help taking down Serge." He looked at me, sorrow in his eyes. "Serge is still a Nightshade wolf, technically. He's my responsibility."

I frowned, remembering how the pack and I had suffered when Conri was alpha. I couldn't think of another pack going through something similar. If we could help, we should. "You have to go."

His eyes widened. "I agree, but not now. Not when we have to prepare to kill Paimon, and to find a cure for your—" He clamped his mouth. He always had a hard time saying it aloud.

"But if you wait, the people will suffer more. Who knows

what will happen? Serge will kill the entire rebel group, then Delco will attack, another war will start … what if Serge kills Delco and becomes alpha of Ironfang too? That will be on our heads too."

"Shit," he muttered.

I rested a hand on his chest, right above his heart. It beat steady and strong. "Go, Shane. I'll be fine. I won't die so soon." He flinched. "Unless Paimon comes up with a surprise attack, we won't attack in at least a few days, not until someone comes up with a good plan." And from what I heard, all the leaders had been disagreeing on how to proceed. That was what happened when there were a dozen, two dozen powerful supernaturals in the same room. "Go, even if it's to assess the situation and create a plan for them. You'll go and come back in no time. Meanwhile, I'll be here, training as much as I can."

Shane wound a strong arm around my waist and pulled me to him. He rested his forehead on mine. "I don't want to stay away from you for one second."

"I know," I whispered. "But like you said, Serge is our responsibility. We can't have him be a tyrant and let an entire pack suffer."

He sighed. "You're right." His arms tightened around me. "I don't want to go, but I should."

I placed a kiss on the tip of his nose. "It'll be okay, Shane. We'll be okay."

The truth was, I was a little nervous about this. What if Serge had gone rabid and Shane got hurt while fighting him? No, I couldn't think about that. I had to believe Shane was stronger and smarter, and his pure heart would be enough to defeat a foul wolf.

A throat cleared a few feet behind us. We turned and saw

a maid placing a large silver tray on a round table. "Here's your lunch. Enjoy," she said, before retreating into the castle.

I stepped away from Shane, but held his hand. "Let's eat. We can continue this conversation after."

14

———

SHANE

THERE WAS NO EASY CONVERSATION AFTER. DURING LUNCH, I made up my mind. As much as it hurt to leave Raika behind, I had to stop Serge. I couldn't be responsible for him torturing, or even massacring, an innocent pack. I never liked Nortrix, and he had allied himself with Paimon, but not everyone there had agreed with their alpha. I had to save them from this.

After lunch, Raika returned to training with the witches, and I went to the village. I met with Killian, Dom, Lucille, Hamill, and Tyren and Hugh.

The moment we were all in the room, I told them right away, "Serge killed the rightful heir of the Whitecrest pack. He's alpha now and he's torturing his people. He's my responsibility and—"

"Was."

I looked at Tyren. "What?"

"He was your responsibility," he continued. "The moment he turned alpha of Whitecrest, he stopped being a Nightshade wolf."

"True, but he only did that because I banished him. It is my fault and my responsibility."

The other wolves nodded.

"Let me guess," Dom said. "You're going to fix this."

I nodded. "And I'm hoping some of you will come with me."

Dom rolled his eyes. "Do you even have to ask?"

"I will gather a handful of my vampires," Killian said, as I thought he would.

I nodded my appreciation.

"I can't go, right?" Tyren asked, looking forlorn.

"Actually, I didn't have the time to ask you yet, but I wanted you to be my second beta," I said. His eyes bugged. "And one beta needs to stay behind and take care of the pack."

"Are you joking?"

"Why would I joke about that?"

A grin spread through his lips. "Cool!"

Cool? That was the answer I got? I chuckled as he and Hugh fist-bumped.

"I can go," Hamill said.

I shook my head. "I would like you here to help Tyren take care of the pack." Tyren lost his smile and frowned. "You're the beta and will be in charge, but Hamill is on the council and has experience. You two will complement each other."

Tyren nodded, though I knew he wasn't entirely happy with it. As much as I wanted to prepare him, I couldn't leave a pack in his hands alone. He would need all the guidance and support he could get.

Lucille sat quietly in a corner, her arms crossed and her mouth turned into a frown.

"Would you like to come with us?"

She gasped, her eyes growing twice their normal size. "Are you serious?"

Her too? "Do I joke around a lot for you all to think I'm joking right now?"

She straightened, her shoulders squared. "Yes! I would love to come with you."

"All right, then pack and get ready." I stood from my chair. "We leave tonight."

I SPENT THE REST OF THE DAY WITH RAIKA. I TOOK SOME BOOKS to the clearing, sat under the shade of a tree, and researched while she trained with Thea and Almae, though I didn't get much done. I was entranced, looking at her being badass. It was fucking sexy.

Thea and Almae conjured several figures to be targets, moving and blinking here and there, and they had different colors. Some even changed colors after the first second, and Raika had to hit them with the right magic.

She turned, twisted, moved her hands with grace and style. With her short shorts, cropped top, boots, and her long hair falling in waves down her back, she looked like a badass goddess.

And she had me wrapped around her finger.

She was killing it.

I left before her practice ended. I needed to take a shower, finish packing, and eat. After I had done all that, I went to the back garden, from where Raika, Thea, and Almae emerged. The witches walked into the castle, while Raika halted before me.

Without a word, I slipped her hand in mine and walked with her to the underground garage. There, two SUVs were being loaded with our bags and with people—Dom, Lucille, Killian, and six of his vampires, including Tao, Louis, and Kalon. Killian had invited Lavinia, but she chose to stay in the castle.

Raika said goodbye to everyone. "Good luck, guys. And please, bring this man back in one piece."

Dom snorted. "I make no promises."

Raika hugged Lucille. "I'm happy for you."

"Me too," Lucille said, way too excited about all of this. Perhaps I shouldn't have invited her.

They all entered the SUVs and I remained outside with Raika.

I turned to her and pulled her to my arms. "Please, be careful," I whispered in her ear.

"You too."

I moved my mouth to hers and kissed her—deep and hard, opening all of my feelings to her. I knew she knew how much I loved her, but it seemed like I needed to show her, tell her all the time.

I pulled back, staring at her beautiful face. "I love you."

Her eyes shone. "I love you too."

I turned, hopped into the SUV's passenger seat, and told Dom to go before I lost the nerve and changed this entire plan.

Dom sped away and I glanced at Raika through the side mirror. She stayed in the same spot until we left the garage and I couldn't see her anymore.

15

RAIKA

Seeing Shane leaving hurt. I stayed in that garage for a long time, trying to force myself to move.

I only did because I had promised to have dinner with Minsi, Tyren, and Rue. Tyren was in an odd mood. He loved being appointed beta, even if he wasn't officially one yet—Shane had to do a small ritual under the moonlight to pass the beta powers to him. However, he was also pissed about not going on the mission.

I was relieved. He was only fifteen. I didn't want him out there fighting yet. By the moon, I hoped that after Shane fixed the problem with Serge and we defeated Paimon, there would be no more fights.

After dinner, I helped Rue in the kitchen, put Minsi to bed, said goodnight to Tyren, and went back to the castle. Once more, while walking away from the village, a sense of loneliness fell over me. I had been alone for so long. I had had only Minsi and Rue for an entire year, and even that had been restricted and controlled. I should be used to being alone, right? But damn, I wasn't anymore. Being alone felt horrible.

A long sigh escaped my lips, and I forced my thoughts to the truth. I might feel alone right now, but that was only because I was walking a deserted path, alone in the dark, and my impeding death hovered over me like a cloudy day.

I knew I wasn't truly alone. All I had to do was say the word and someone would come to me. Or they would let me come to them—my family, Rue, Lavinia, Thea, Almae. Even Lucille, though she wasn't here now.

My thoughts turned to Ivy. While I had been with her and Paimon, she had been a good friend, a great sister. I missed her.

My phone vibrated, and I pulled it out from my back pocket.

I skidded to a stop and stared at the screen.

I need your help.

It was from an unknown number, but for some reason, I knew who this was.

Ivy?

Yeah. It's me. Can we meet?

I frowned. Was this really Ivy? I had tossed the other phone away and I hadn't added Ivy's number to this one. She could also have changed it. If I was a higher demon on the run, I probably would change phones every couple of weeks, or I would only use burners.

I called her, but she didn't pick up.

Ivy: *I can't talk right now. Text is safer.*

Me: *How do I know it's you?*

Ivy: *Are you doubting your own sister?*

Me: *Well, you tried to kill me.*

Ivy: *No, I didn't. I couldn't even hurt you.*

That was the damn truth and why I thought of her often.

Me: *What do you want?*

Ivy: *I'm on the run. I left our father, but he's not a compassionate man and is hunting me. I don't think I can keep running from him much longer.*

I sucked in a sharp breath.

Me: *And you want me to do what?*

Ivy: *I thought ... the safest place would be to go to you, but I'm afraid of your friends. If I try to get close, they will kill me on the spot.*

I wouldn't let them do that, but I wouldn't give in so easily.

Me: *So?*

Ivy: *Meet me somewhere safe, neutral. Let's talk. I'll let you try to convince me to come back with you, even if I might end up in a cell. Or you can help me figure out how to hide from Paimon.*

Me: *Why can't you do that on your own?*

I flinched at my own words. I didn't mean to be so harsh, but I had to know what her game was here.

Ivy: *I could try. I'm not as strong as our father. But you are. With your power, you could create a spell to hide me. No?*

I shook my head. Spell from dragon magic? Was that something she knew from living with Paimon? I would have to try that later. But for now ...

Me: *I don't know.*

Ivy: *Please, Raika. You know how much I hate begging. It's not my style. But you're my sister and I thought we had bonded.*

We had. I hated she wasn't on the right side.

Me: *Give me a few minutes. I need to think about this.*

Not really. Despite everything, despite knowing this could be a trap, I couldn't sit here and ignore her. Ivy was my sister and I knew she wasn't as bad as Paimon. Not even close.

If I told anyone about it, they wouldn't let me go after her. No, they would send a team to check on her. She wouldn't show up then, and I would miss my opportunity to talk to her, to bring her on to this side.

I rushed to my bedroom, changed my shorts to leggings, and my crop top to a tank top, picked up a jacket, grabbed a bag with a few essentials (mainly, lots of elixir), and stared at my phone.

Holy shit, was I really doing this?

This was messed up. I should stay, go to sleep, wake up early tomorrow morning, and train with Thea and Almae. When they found out I was gone, they would hunt me down, and when they found me, they would skin me alive.

Oh, Shane ... he would be so disappointed in me.

But this was Ivy. My sister. An almost friend. I knew she wasn't bad, and I knew we could be much more. If I could get her away from Paimon, I had to do it. I had to try. She deserved a better life.

I pushed everything else to the back of my mind, otherwise I would chicken out. I slung my bag across my shoulder and left my room. I walked normally through the hallways. It was late, but not too late. Most vampires and witches were still awake. I crossed by two vampire guards and they paid no attention to me. Good.

I went to the underground garage, more specifically, to the small mudroom before exiting into it, where all the car keys were hanging from hooks on the wall. There had to be at least fifty keys here, for the fifty plus cars parked here. I glanced out, saw which car was the smallest—an Audi A3— and looked for its keys.

I grabbed it, entered the car, and prayed it remained quiet while I drove out of the garage, down the long driveway, and out onto the road. The engine purred to life, like a quiet cat. I drove the car away, glad no one stopped me.

I was sure some guards saw the car leaving the garage, even if they might not have recognized the driver. As I turned onto the highway off the castle's property, I was sure that Drake and Thea had been informed of the "stolen" car and were trying to determine who was driving.

It was a matter of time until they figured out it was me.

I stopped the car at the shoulder and texted Ivy.

Where should I meet you?

By the moon, I hoped she didn't tell me something like Chicago or Los Angeles. I didn't want to have to get a flight to go meet her.

She sent me the address of a motel not even four hours from DuMoir. I let out a relieved breath and entered the address on the car's GPS. Then, I drove in silence for the next four hours.

***

Not an hour after I left, my cell phone vibrated. I glanced at the first texts and calls that came—Lavinia and Thea. After a while, even that bothered me, so I turned my phone off.

I felt bad about it, but I knew that if I answered or replied, they would try to talk me out of this, and I couldn't back off now.

At least, they couldn't tell Shane I was missing, not while he was on an overnight flight to the other side of the continent. Hopefully, they wouldn't tell him at all, or he would be distracted.

A pang cut through my chest. I hated lying to him. He would be pissed with me when he came back.

Everyone would.

Again, I shook my head. No, I couldn't think about Shane or our friends right now. Right now, the only thing that matter was getting to Ivy.

I arrived at the shady motel at almost two in the morning. There were only two cars in the parking lot—the black sedan Ivy had mentioned was parked in the far back.

I slowed my car beside hers, glancing at the inn. On the second floor, a figure looked out from a window. The bright light was right behind her and I couldn't see her face, but I knew that was Ivy. She gestured for me to come over.

If this was a trap, would Ivy participate willingly? Or was Paimon holding her hostage, asking her to send me those messages?

There was only one way to know.

With a sigh, I grabbed my bag from the passenger seat, slung it across my shoulders, and headed toward the inn. As I walked to the second floor, I glanced around for any signs of danger. If there were demons hidden in the darkness beyond the inn, I wouldn't know, would I?

A sudden dread coursed through me. This was a really bad idea, but I was here now, and I couldn't turn and leave without knowing if this was really Ivy. I couldn't bear the thought that it could really be her and leaving her behind.

So, instead of panicking, I rolled my shoulders and thought of what I could say to her to convince her to come back with me. Jitters ran through my arms as I raised my hand to knock on the door.

It opened before I could touch it.

I walked into the dim room, holding the door open. "Ivy?" I looked around.

She sat in the armchair across the room. Relief relaxed my muscles. It was really her.

I closed the door and took a couple of steps closer.

Then I really saw her.

Her mouth gagged, her hands tied, and her eyes wild.

I froze.

"Hello, Raika," a familiar voice said from behind me, a colder tone than I remembered.

Slowly, I turned around.

And faced my father, the former prince of the underworld.

Fear closed my throat.

A wicked grin took over his lips. "I'm so glad you came."

"I can't say the same." I called on both my magics, but a sudden jolt froze me in place. Panic rose in my chest.

Paimon lifted his finger and moved it side to side. "Nu-uh, you can't fight me."

I didn't want to fight him, not right now. I focused on both my magics and brought them to the surface. With a loud pop, his hold on me broke.

"Come on, Ivy." I reached for her and my arm went through her as she became smoke right in front of my eyes. I stilled. "What's this?"

"You didn't think I would bring her here, did you?"

"What was that, then?" I pointed to where Ivy had just been. "An illusion?"

"Not an illusion," he said, sounding proud of himself. "What you saw was the real Ivy, but she isn't here. Let's say it was a mirror spell. She was watching us too."

She wasn't here? Where was she?

In the realm, the one Paimon now held the key to.

If I wanted Ivy, I would have to go there.

But he couldn't know I wanted that.

I brought my hands up, threw a bolt of darkfire right at him, and ran for the door. He easily dodged it and turned to me.

"You can't run from me!" he practically shouted.

"Want to bet?" I threw the door open and dashed out.

And right through a green portal.

MY HEART LEAPT TO MY THROAT AS I SCANNED MY surroundings.

"Do you like it?" Paimon asked, once again right behind me. Of course, he had cheated and put a portal in my path. Well, less work for me. I thought I would have to run from him for a few minutes before letting him take me.

I looked around.

We were in ... I didn't even know what to call this place. We stood on a wide ledge of an enormous cavern. Ten feet to my right the ledge ended. I leaned a little, trying to get a look at what was below, but all I saw was infinite darkness. Looking up, I saw more ledges and passages, bridges, all made of stone, as if carved directly from the rocks.

Many stories above, a thin cut in the stone let light in. Mirrors of varying sizes hung along the rocks, purposely positioned to spread the light.

"Are we inside a mountain?" I asked, confused.

"Something like that," Paimon answered.

I turned and looked at him. I inhaled sharply. Now that we weren't in that dim room, I could see him again, and I had forgotten how stoic and intimidating he was. His entire being exuded power and violence, and I wanted to cower in his presence.

"Are we on Earth?" I asked, my voice low.

Paimon shoved his hand in the pockets of his suit pants. "No. We are in the Huddyria realm. It's a beautiful place, and though it looks a little primitive in its architecture, they have advances in magic that we have never seen."

I inhaled sharply. "You're using them. They are your army."

Paimon clicked his tongue. "Despite the many offers I made them, they do not want to lend me their army, only a small squadron. Though, for a crazy amount of money, they are letting me use their portal to come and go as I please. It's very convenient."

I frowned. Why was he answering my question? Because he was telling me a lie so I could tell the others and trick us again? Or because he had no plans to let me walk out of here?

I was betting on the latter.

Paimon looked down the abyss. "You know, this clan believes there's a monster, even uglier and nastier than them, living in the depths of this mountain? They think that one day, it'll crawl from the darkness and eat them all."

I frowned. That was stupid. Then why didn't they leave this mountain? I shook my head, clearing my thoughts. I focused on what was important.

"Where's Ivy?"

Paimon walked around me. "That is not how this game works."

"So this is a game?"

"Perhaps. I could put my hands around your neck and take your magic away, but what is the fun in that?"

I thought he had a more nefarious plan for me, like using me as bait to lure the others and attack them while he sneaked through the gate.

"All you want is my power?"

His eyes flashed dark. "Every ounce of it."

I gulped.

"Didn't I tell you what I did to your siblings when they didn't want to join me? I absorbed their magic. Most died in the process, and those who didn't ..." He shrugged. "I killed them after."

I shuddered and my stomach revolved. "You told me."

"When your dear mate rescued you, I considered letting you go. But then you had to show up when we were killing the dragon, didn't you?" His face grew red and he shouted, "And you stole half of my magic!" I winced. Paimon took a deep breath and smoothed his hands over his suit jacket. "That magic is mine, and I'll have it."

He lifted his hands, lunging for me.

I created a wall of dragon's magic between us. "Hear me out!"

He halted.

"Let me see Ivy. Let me have a few moments with her, as sisters. If I confirm she is fine and taken care of, I'll surrender. I'll let you have the dragon's magic. Hell, you can even have the darkfire." I never wanted any of those magics. All I wanted was to be a wolf shifter and be welcomed in my pack —one I was born like, the other I had achieved on my own.

Paimon tilted his head, narrowed his eyes at me. "That easy?"

"That easy," I lied. As if I would surrender to this demon. I just needed to get to Ivy. Then I would think of a second part to this crazy plan.

"All right," he said.

I dropped the shield

"To show you I appreciate when you lived with me, I'll let you see Ivy for the rest of the night. In the morning, you'll come to me." He snapped his fingers.

Two figures walked from the archway along the rocks, and I took a step back from the tall humanoids with yellowish, sleek skin, broad shoulders, a long nose, claws, and razor teeth.

"This is your first time seeing a Huddyriun, isn't it?" He chuckled. "Don't worry, they won't hurt you unless I tell them to."

I swallowed my disgust and fear as they wrapped big hands around my arms and pulled me with them.

We were about to cross the archway into the darkness, when Paimon called, "Oh, Raika." The Huddyriuns stopped and turned me to face the demon again. "Do you think this was all a coincidence? Your mate suddenly needs to travel thousands of miles away from you, and then you get a text from Ivy?"

The blood drained from my face. "You ... you did that."

"I did, and it was satisfying." He put his hands in his pockets again and rolled on the balls of his feet. "If it all works out, that will be the last you see of him."

He turned his back to me and the Huddyriuns pulled a numb me into the dark tunnel.

16

SHANE

WE DROVE TO A REGIONAL AIRPORT, AND GOT A CHARTERED flight to Prince Albert, Saskatchewan. We slept through the six-hour flight, and when we arrived at the airport, we rented two cars and drove north, to the Whitecrest pack lands.

Eike agreed to meet us at the Nightshade's main square. "No one goes that way anymore," he said.

The sun was rising on the horizon as we entered the pack lands, shining a soft golden light over the forest. We drove down the main road, a pang cut through my chest. This had been my home and now it was—

"Stop the car," I said.

Killian slammed the breaks. "What is it?"

I pushed the door open, hopping out of the car. Stunned, I stared at the forest flanking the road.

Killian, Dom, and Lucille stepped behind me. The other car also stopped and Tao lowered the window. "What's going on?"

"Shane, talk to me," Killian said.

Dom inhaled a sharp breath. "The land."

I nodded and looked at him with huge eyes. "Right."

"Oh," Killian said. "The land was poisoned here, wasn't it?"

But it wasn't anymore. No, the forest was as green and abundant as I remembered. Thick and vibrant trees, full bushes, colorful flowers went on forever, and the sweet and woody scent floated in the air. I turned around, taking everything in. Perhaps when the crystal had been destroyed after the dragon woke up, the poison disappeared.

A sliver of hope snaked through my chest.

No, I couldn't think like that. The town was destroyed by the fire. There was no way for us to fix that.

With a sigh, I returned to the car. "Let's go."

Silent, the others joined me inside the car, and we drove to the square. The buildings were a broken skeleton of what they used to be, and the entire town was black with soot and ash. Even if we wanted to come back, it would take us months, if not years, to rebuild it all.

We stopped the cars along Main Street as Eike appeared from the other end of the road, flanked by the two wolves who had been with him before.

We hopped out of the car and went to meet with him.

Right in front of the library, we stood and faced each other.

"Eike," I said by way of greeting.

"Thank you for coming, Shane," Eike said, his voice low. He averted his gaze.

I frowned. Last time I was here, Eike hadn't cowered or seemed insecure. Something was wrong. "Eike, what is going on?"

Laughter filled the street.

Serge.

Rage filled my veins as he strolled closer, with a dozen of wolves behind him—two of his old buddies and the rest from Whitecrest.

I clenched my fists. "What's going on?"

"Hello, Shane." Serge halted beside Eike. "Isn't this a happy surprise? Aren't you glad to see me?"

I gritted my teeth. "Only if I can kill you." I glared at Eike. "You tricked me!"

"It wasn't his fault," Serge said. He snapped his fingers. From behind his men, two wolves pushed a female forward. She stumbled on her feet and almost faceplanted. Eike flinched, but the two wolves caught her arm and pulled her back roughly. "I have his mate."

It dawned on me. "You used her to make him call me here."

"Bingo." Serge clapped his hands three times. "I can't take all the credit, though."

"What do you mean?"

"It was my idea," a new voice came from our left. I looked at the man and instantly remembered him.

"Rotgar." He was Paimon's demon, his right hand.

Wearing a suit, the demon walked closer as if he didn't have a care in the entire world. "Precisely."

A little confusion mixed with my rage. "What the hell are you doing here?"

Rotgar looked at his manicured nails. "Do you think Serge is smart or strong enough to take over the Whitecrest pack?"

"Hey!" Serge snapped.

Rotgar didn't even look his way. He kept his impassive dark eyes on me.

"You helped him," I said. The demon nodded. "Why?"

"Ah, it isn't fun when it's this easy. Try to guess."

I frowned. This piece of shit wanted to play games with me? I was already tired of this. "Just get it over with," I snarled.

"I helped Serge, because we knew you would feel obligated and come running to fix this mess." We. My face fell. It couldn't be ... "Right, I see it in your eyes." He snapped his fingers. "You know why we wanted you here."

Fur rolled down my arms, and my hands shifted into claws. "What did you do?"

Rotgar shrugged. "I didn't do anything. Paimon, on the other hand, by now, has Raika within his clutches, and if he hasn't taken her magic yet, he's about to."

It couldn't be.

"Shane, he's goading you," Killian whispered.

"Right, don't fall for it," Dom said, equally low. "Raika is at the castle."

Was she? My fingers itched to get my phone and call her, but I couldn't lose focus of the people around me right now. If I got distracted, it would be the end of us.

That was exactly what he was trying to do, right? He was making me upset, spewing ridiculous lies so I would fall prey to my rage.

No, I was better than this.

"Say whatever you want, I'm not falling for that," I told him.

Rotgar shrugged. "Whatever you want. It's not like you can do anything from here, right?" A growl started in my chest. "Oh, wait, I almost forgot. I've invited another guest to this party."

Footsteps sounded behind us.

I turned and inhaled sharply. Delco and a dozen of Ironfang wolves walked toward us. By the moon, this had to get better and better, didn't it?

Our group retreated, opening up the circle—hell if I would be stuck between Serge and Delco. This way, I had one on my right, and one on my left.

Delco halted a good ways from us. "Hello, Shane."

I snarled. "What are you doing here?"

He stared at me. "You didn't honor my request."

His request. When Nortrix challenged me, Delco asked for me to lose. He wanted me to let Nortrix kill me, otherwise, the Ironfang would start a war with the Nightshade.

I frowned. "You probably know Nortrix didn't show up for the challenge, and even if he had, I wouldn't let him kill me to satisfy you."

Delco bared his fangs. "Then that means war."

He whistled and his men shifted. A beat later, Serge's lackeys shifted.

They all attacked.

I shifted before they got to me. Dom did the same, and Killian and his vampires zoomed into the fight.

A wolf jumped for me, but I dodged his attack and dove to the side. I twisted my body and closed my mouth around his shoulder. I buried my teeth deep and pulled, ripping muscle and flesh. The wolf howled. I dropped him, and he fell into a lifeless pile.

I turned away from him, looking for Rotgar.

His dark eyes met mine from across the fight, near the infirmary's corner. With a snarl, I ran after him. I weaved through the fight, avoiding direct strikes and jumping over fallen bodies. I got to the infirmary, turning in a circle. The demon was gone. I sniffed the air, the ground, but there was no hint of his scent anywhere. It was like he had opened a portal and gone through.

Frustration coursed through me, and I turned to the two men still holding Eike's mate captive. Their gazes were on Eike and Serge, who were circling each other not far from them, but not attacking. Using their distraction, I moved behind them and struck. The two went down before they could utter a word. Eike's mate gave me a sharp nod, then shifted, joining the fight.

I needed to end this madness fast.

Delco stood back, still in his human form, watching everyone. What the hell was he waiting for? I pushed him out of my mind and focused on Eike and Serge.

I jumped to Eike's side, snarling at Serge. The wolf seemed to peel his lips back in a grin. He wouldn't be smiling for too long.

They continued circling each other and not doing anything, and I was sick of this. I lunged for Serge. He jumped to the side, and thankfully, Eike got the hint and moved, rushing into Serge from the other side. He snapped his teeth, inches from Serge's neck, but the wolf was like a snake, slithering out of the way. I jumped on his back and held him down. Then, I howled at Eike.

Eike pressed a paw on Serge's muzzle, pushing it toward the ground and clamped his teeth around his throat. Serge struggled, but with the both of us holding him. There was nothing he could do. Eike bit down and jerked to the side. A sickening crack echoed.

I pulled back.

Eike let out a howl. The Whitecrest wolves who had come with Serge stopped fighting. They all turned to Delco and his wolves. The Ironfang wolves formed a line before their alpha.

The coward stared at me, then turned to leave. Oh, no, he wouldn't. I yelped once. Instantly, the vampires surrounded Delco and the Whitecrest wolves attacked the Ironfang pack.

"For wolves' sake," he muttered before taking off his shirt and shifting into an impressive brown wolf. He snapped at the vampires, but they didn't fight him. They were there to hold the Ironfang's alpha back.

I entered the circle formed by the vampires with Eike by my side. We weren't in the same pack and couldn't communicate through the pack's link, but when he looked at me, I saw he understood what I wanted him to do. What my suggestion was.

He let out a low yelp and lunged at Delco. I stayed there, watching the fight. If needed, I would interfere. I would hold Delco down so Eike could get to him. I was tired of these tyrant alphas, and if the Ironfang and the Whitecrest had to unite under one flag, then so be it.

But I didn't have to do anything.

Surrounded by vampires, and with me there, Delco didn't have anywhere to run. Eike tricked him when he jumped right, rolled left, and lunged from behind, closing his mouth on Delco's shoulder. The Ironfang alpha went down and didn't get up anymore.

Eike howled and the Ironfang wolves stopped, their heads low.

We shifted back, our bodies sweaty and stained with blood. I looked around. One of our vampires was done, another two were badly hurt, but would probably be all right, and at least another five wolves had died in this senseless battle.

I was so fucking tired of this.

"That's not what I wanted," Eike said. His eyes scanned

the scene like I had done. "I had to call you because he had my mate." He extended his hand and his mate stepped closer, slipping her hand in his. "You have a mate. I know you would do anything for her."

I nodded. "I would."

"Forgive me," he whispered.

"All that I ask is that you lead both packs as one with dignity and honor. Be a good alpha and this—" I gestured to the blood and body around us. "—won't happen ever again."

He nodded. "I will do my best."

"Good." I looked at my friends. Several yards back, Dom talked to one of the Ironfang wolves, a female with long, brown curls. I frowned. What was that about?

Killian picked up a bag from one of the cars. "Get dressed." He threw me jeans and a shirt. "Then let's take care of the bodies and go." He threw clothes at Lucille, then he walked to Dom, who still was talking to the brunette.

I shoved my pants, then patted my pockets. My phone wasn't here. I rushed to the car, picked up my phone, and called Raika. It was ten in the morning here, so it should be noon in Connecticut. She was probably on a break from training and eating lunch with the witches. The phone went to voice message.

What the hell?

I tried calling again. Nothing.

I called Drake. He answered on the third ring, "I knew you would call sooner or later."

"Because you know I probably called Raika and she didn't answer. What happened?"

Two beats passed. "Raika is missing."

17

RAIKA

THEY TOOK ME THROUGH A SERIES OF WIDE TUNNELS THAT wound up and down the mountain. Torches lined the rough walls every few feet, though instead of flames, there were small white gems on top, and they shone as bright as an LED light.

It was beautiful, but eerie.

I tried keeping tabs of where we were going, where to turn, but all my mind wanted to focus on was the fact that Paimon orchestrated all of this—taking Shane away so I would fall for his trap without any hesitation.

And now Shane was in even more danger because of me.

We entered a wider hallway lined with thick doors. I couldn't identify the material, but it shone like metal but had the texture of wood.

The Huddyriuns stopped at one of the doors in the middle of the hallway. One of them took a heavy key from the hook on his belt, unlocked it, and pushed it open. He shoved me inside, then locked the door behind me.

"Raika!" I barely saw anything before Ivy lunged at me.

She hugged me tight. "You stupid woman. Why did you come? Didn't you know it was a trap?"

I pulled back, looking at her. Her hair was a mess, there were dark circles under her eyes, and she looked way too thin and frail. "Aren't they feeding you?"

She snorted and walked back. "Only enough so I don't die."

I frowned and looked around. We were in a tiny room with the same rough walls I had seen all over this place. The same gem from the hallways hung from the ceiling, illuminating the room, especially the uneven ceiling. There was a cot on the left side, a chair and a small table to the right, and an archway on the back, which led somewhere. A bathroom? And that was it. No windows, nothing.

"How long have you been here?"

She plopped down the chair and rubbed at her wrist. She had been tied up moments ago, hadn't she? Anger bubbled inside of me.

"A couple of days after you and Father got the dragon magic," she said, her voice somber. "I tried to run and he caught me, of course. He said my plan was great, but I was using it wrong." She gestured to us. "And here we are. He used it to bring you here."

"That's why he didn't kill you?" She winced at my words. "Sorry, I didn't mean to be so callous. It's just ... he mentioned before, to have killed and absorbed the magic from our siblings who didn't want to join him."

"I know. I've seen him do it, you know, and each time it made me sick. But what could I do? I was never powerful enough to stop him."

"That's why you joined him? Because you didn't want to die?"

"What's up with all the questions?"

"I'm trying to understand, that's all."

She was quiet for a second, and I thought she wouldn't answer me. "That, and because he was the worst bully. I'm one of the only pure-blooded demons he sired, which means I'm more powerful than others. He really wanted me working by his side. He threatened my mother." She paused. "She was killed by a group of angels a couple of years later."

I knew how it felt to lose a mother. "I'm sorry."

"I was so deep into Paimon's shit, I couldn't see a way out. I knew what he did to our siblings. So I pretended I was okay with all of it. Fake it until you make it. I tried but never quite got to that part."

"I'm sorry," I repeated. It was terrible that she had to live through all of that, but it was also a relief to know she was never like him.

"It's not your fault. I should have been braver." She sighed. "But yes, to answer one of your million questions, I think he was keeping me alive to lure you to us. Now you're here and he'll kill the both of us tomorrow."

No, I wouldn't allow that.

I picked up my phone from my bag and cursed again. Of course it wouldn't work here. We were on another realm, for the moon's sake! I clenched my hands. "Shit." I sat at the edge of the bed, defeated. "This is worse than I thought it would be."

"What do you mean?"

"I knew this was a trap from the beginning," I said. "I mean, I hoped it wasn't, but I was sure it was. All I wanted was to get to you so we both could bust out of wherever he was holding you."

"We are in another realm. Even if we can bust out of here, we still need the key to open the portal."

"Exactly. I kind forgot to take that into consideration when I thought of my plan." Now, I felt utterly stupid because of it. I knew Paimon had been coming and going to another realm. Why didn't I think he would keep Ivy there?

"I'm sorry," she whispered. "You came because of me."

I stared at her. "Do you really want to leave him?" She nodded. "To do what?"

She shrugged. "Anything that doesn't involve killing, robbing, or criminal activity. I might sell my properties, buy a desert island, and spend the rest of my days drinking margaritas on the beach."

That did sound lovely, but lonely. "How about we start by getting out of here? Then we can plan for a better future."

"We're stuck in some kind of cell, deep inside a mountain, in a strange realm full of ugly creatures," she mused. "How in the hell will we escape this place?"

"We use our smarts, along with our magic, and bust out."

She rolled her eyes. "Again with busting out of here?"

"Do you have a better idea?"

She stared at me, her blue eyes shining bright. "No."

"Then, let's get to work. We need a plan."

There wasn't much to do in Ivy's room-slash-cell other than wait. She told me she probably wouldn't receive any food until the morning (they were following Earth's twenty-four hour day here), and that was probably when Paimon would come back to get me.

We needed to act then.

The first hour was awkward. We remained in silence, and at some point, Ivy lay down on the cot and slept. I was getting sleepy too, but I didn't trust myself to sleep. After we escaped, I could rest. For now, I needed to be sharp, but I let Ivy sleep. She was probably weak from eating so little, and sick of being stuck in this tiny room, which made her more exhausted.

I sat on the floor in a meditating position and tried to focus. We could do this. I didn't know how, but we could do this.

I grabbed an elixir from my bag. It was still the middle of the night, and we had a couple of hours to go. It was better if I drank it now and be prepared for a fight later.

"What is that?" Ivy asked, sitting up in bed.

I frowned. "First, answer this: How's Paimon fairing with the dragon's magic? Any side effects?"

She shook her head. "I ... I don't know. I've been locked away since after he got the magic. I have no idea what's going on. Why?"

"Well, my body can't handle the dragon's magic." I told her about losing control right in the beginning, exploding into flames, and what the elixir did for me. I also told her the dragon's magic wasn't made for a supernatural like me. "It's killing me."

Her eyes widened. "What? But there's a cure, right?"

I shook my head. "Not that we know of, though plenty of witches are researching, trying to find something." But I had no hope they would succeed. All the information we had about dragons and dragon shifters was almost a thousand years old. We practically knew nothing about them.

She stared at me with such misery in her eyes. "There has to be something."

"Careful. I'll think you care."

"I do care. Everything we lived through together, our conversations, our good times, that was real. I know you might not believe me, but it was. You're my sister and I care about you."

I looked up at the light, not wanting to cry now. No, I was about to fight a bunch of demons and those ugly Huddyri-uns. I had no time to cry.

I cleared my throat. "We still have a couple more hours to go, you should go back to sleep." I extended my legs in front of me and tried reaching my toes. I should get my body ready for the fight to come.

"What about you? You should sleep too."

I shook my head. "I won't be able to sleep now."

"I don't think I can sleep anymore either." She sat down beside me and started stretching too.

A couple of hours went by. Ivy and I stretched for a long time, took a break, stretched again. As the time passed, I could feel the effects of the elixir lessening. Soon, I would be at the perfect point where the dragon's magic wasn't numb, but it wasn't unstable either, and I could do whatever I wanted with it.

I checked the time on my dying phone for the thousandth time. "It's almost seven."

"Then they will be here soon," Ivy said.

She sat on the cot and I took the chair.

Seven came and went, and no one showed up.

Ivy's heels bounced up and down. "Something's wrong."

"Or Paimon is playing with us," I mused. At least, that was what I was telling myself. "He wants to make us concerned. Agitated." I gave her a pointed look and she stilled her leg.

A little after nine, the door finally opened and a demon

appeared at the doorway. Rotgar, Paimon's general and most trusted demon. He looked over at us with disdain.

Ivy frowned. "Where's my breakfast?"

"You won't need your breakfast today," he said with a small grin. "Or ever." He gestured for us to get up. "Now come on."

Ivy and I exchanged a look. She was the first to stand, following him out. With my bag across my shoulders, I followed them out, and realized why Rotgar was so nonchalant. Because there were a dozen demons plus four Huddyriuns here to escort us to Paimon. If we tried anything now, we wouldn't get far.

The group took us to the same ledge as before, and now I actually paid attention to it. To the left, the ledge opened to a bigger room where there were couches, rugs, a long table, and housewares.

Paimon stood in that room, his back to us. When he turned around with a glass of whiskey in his hand, he smiled wide at us. "My daughters." He sipped from his drink and walked toward us.

The demons and Huddyriuns spread out through the ledge, forming a wide arc around Ivy and me. All right, I hadn't predicted our odds. Two against seventeen was pretty bad.

Shit.

No, I wouldn't give up hope yet.

Paimon stopped a few feet from us. "Did you have a good night?"

Ivy stared at him with pure hatred in her eyes. "As if you care."

Paimon nodded. "True, but I'm a prince." He opened one

arm wide, as if showing himself. "I'm polite. Thus the question."

"Just get to it," I said through gritted teeth.

Ivy shot me an are-you-crazy look. Well, what did she want? Standing here and waiting for whatever wasn't going to change the outcome. We had no help other than ourselves, and the only thing that could happen was for Paimon to call more of his allies to watch the show.

"First, Rotgar needs to report to me," Paimon said.

Rotgar's lip curled. "The Whitecrest and the Ironfang are attacking Shane and his friends as we speak."

The blood rushed from my face. "What?"

"I was there personally." Rotgar sounded proud. "I've brought them all together, poked them, and let them loose." He shrugged. "I just came back." He handed Paimon the portal key.

With a smile, Paimon placed the key on the inside pocket of his suit, just above his dead heart. "Isn't that good news?"

No, they were the worst. Rotgar had led Shane into an ambush ... and now I was in another one. We both had fallen into this mess.

Paimon drank the rest of his whiskey, then threw the glass over the ledge. We never heard the glass breaking.

"All right, if you're so eager to die." His lips turned up. "Ivy, you're first." He reached for her.

Ivy stepped back, but the demons pushed her forward. Paimon walked to her. She struggled, but went still when he closed his hand around her neck.

Paimon inhaled deeply and her eyes widened.

Shit. It was now or never.

I didn't think; I acted.

As fast as I could, I called my magic. I threw a wave of darkfire toward the demons and Huddyriuns, going around the room and taking them down like dominos—most fell from the ledge to the abyss. Their screams echoed through the cavern.

Then, I created a wall of dragon magic between Ivy and Paimon. He hissed when the wall closed around his wrists and he pulled back. His eyes turned red, but before he could retaliate, I pushed the wall to him. It hit him and exploded, making him stumble back.

I lunged at him, grabbing the collar of his suit and shoving him down. "Now, Ivy!"

She jumped into action and conjured darkfire cuffs around his wrists and ankles. We knew that wouldn't hold him long. Two seconds later, dragon magic burst from Paimon. It hit me hard, taking my breath away. I fell back on the rough stone, pain spreading over my back.

Groaning, I rolled to the side.

"You, insolent bitch," he snarled, looking at me. Ivy threw darkfire at him. That made him look at her. "You too."

The handful of demons who remained at the ledge were getting up from their daze, and I didn't have much time to act. Rotgar was one of them.

I pushed to my feet. "Hey!"

Paimon stopped and looked at me. Ivy rushed to my side. "I promise you one thing: you won't win."

The key in my hand glowed green—I had snatched it from Paimon when I tackled him to the ground—and a portal appeared behind Ivy and me. We ran.

"No!" Paimon screamed.

Ivy and I jumped through the portal. My feet barely touched the ground when something yanked at my head, pulling me back. I yelped. Paimon had grabbed my hair.

"Come back here!"

Half of his arm was through the portal, the other half was still back in the other realm. With his other hand, he took the key from me and tugged me to come with him.

I kicked him in the chest. At first, he held on to my hair, and I screamed as pain spread through my head, but then he let go. He fell back into the portal.

It closed.

I fell to my knees, breathing hard. We had made it. I had rescued Ivy and now we were back on Earth, back at the motel—it had happened so fast, that was the first place that had come to mind.

Ivy crouched beside me. "Are you okay?"

I looked down at myself. My head hurt from the hair pulling, and I had lost the portal key. But otherwise, I was okay. More than okay, I had her back.

I nodded. "Yeah, but we should go. He has the key and he can come back at any second."

I grabbed her hand and together, we ran to the car and sped away from there.

18

RAIKA

"WE'RE ALMOST THERE," I TOLD IVY.

She groaned.

After we left the inn behind, Ivy asked me to drop her off anywhere. As if I would. I was bringing her to DuMoir Castle.

"They will kill me on sight!"

"No, they won't," I said. "I won't allow it." And I believed that. My friends could be fearsome and powerful supernaturals but they weren't monsters. They didn't kill without a good reason.

I would make Ivy's case.

We stopped once for gas, food, and a potty break, and Ivy actually tried to ditch me. I had to yell at her just outside the gas station. People probably thought we were crazy and were about to call the police, but then she relented and came with me.

During the drive's last thirty minutes, I drank another elixir and turned on my phone. Instantly, I regretted it when dozens of texts and missed calls flooded the screen. "Shit."

"Looks like someone is in trouble," Ivy said, as if enjoying this.

"Just ... call Thea. Please." I shoved my phone into her hands. She pressed on Thea's name and started the call. The phone rang in the car's speakers.

"Raika!" Thea answered, sounding both mad and relieved. "Where the hell are you?"

"I'll be at the castle soon. I wanted to tell you ... I have a guest."

"A guest?"

"I'm bringing Ivy with me."

"You subdued her?"

"No, she's coming willingly. I'm telling you so you don't attack her. She's not here to fight."

"You know we won't be able to invite her in."

I glanced at Ivy. She gave me a sad nod. "I know. We know."

"All right. I'll tell Drake and prepare for your arrival."

"Good. Thanks." I reached my finger to the dashboard, to turn off the call.

"Oh, and Raika? Shane is possessed." Shit. Of course that by now he knew something was going on. "He's probably on the flight back and won't be able to answer if you call, but you could at least send him a message so he sees it first thing when the flight lands, hm?"

I sighed. "Will do."

"Okay. I'll see you soon." She turned off the call.

"Trouble in paradise?" Ivy asked, still holding my phone.

I gave her a side glance. Not long ago, Ivy had been my best friend. In the two weeks that I had spent with her, believing she had always been there for me, I had felt a connection with her I had never felt before. Would it hurt if I let her in a little?

"There's no trouble, just ... some concern."

Ivy's brows curled down. "Shane is probably on edge because you're dying."

My eyes rounded. "Exactly."

"He doesn't know what you did, does he?"

I shook my head. "Paimon created a distraction back at our pack lands so Shane would be away." I wouldn't have any qualms about sneaking off on him. Though I would have tried to convince him to help me first.

"Typical," Ivy muttered.

I looked at her again. She had known Paimon her entire life, and lived with him for a couple of years now, and he could be manipulative. When with him, you believed whatever he wanted you to believe. It was incredible and sickening at the same time.

If Ivy was deeply ensnared in his web, it wasn't entirely her fault.

It was past two in the afternoon when I turned the car onto the castle's private road. Ivy glanced around, taking in the extensive lawn, the beautiful gardens, the village on the far side, the moon-shaped lake, and then the castle.

"The famous DuMoir Castle," she whispered. "And its reception."

I didn't even bother turning into the underground garage because, as expected, a crowd came to receive us in front of the castle. I slowed down the car and stopped right beside the stairs leading to the massive front door.

I grabbed Ivy's wrist. "They won't be nice to you, at least not yet. But don't worry. They won't hurt you unless provoked."

She nodded.

We exited the car and the crowd surrounded us.

Drake, Thea, Almae, Lavinia, Elisa, and Zadkiel were right beside the car, their eyes trained on Ivy.

"Welcome to DuMoir Castle, Ivy," Drake said, his voice tight. "Unfortunately, I can't offer you a tour or anything of the sort, but I can offer you comfortable accommodations while we sort this out." Drake gestured to the door behind them.

Ivy glanced at me. I gave her one short nod. With a sigh, she stepped forward.

"Just a small warning," Thea said as Ivy walked by her. "Try anything and we'll respond in measure."

Ivy held her head high. "I'm not here to fight."

Thea nodded. "Good."

"Please, follow me," Elisa said, taking the lead.

We were a procession walking through the castle's corridors. First, Elisa and Zadkiel, with two vampire guards on their sides. Next was Ivy, with four guards flanking her. Then the rest of us.

As we crossed intersections and other hallways, I saw guards stationed at every turn and corner, something I had not seen before in the castle.

Elisa guided us to the guest wing on the second floor. She stopped in front of the last door in the long hallway. She opened it and stepped back, gesturing for Ivy to go in.

Ivy hesitate for a brief second, then marched inside the room. I followed her in, along with Thea and Drake. She turned around in a circle, taking in the room. It looked like most guest bedrooms in the castle: expensive rugs, heavy curtains over the large windows, a queen bed to one side, and a loveseat, two armchairs, and coffee table to the other. A door opened to a short walk-in closet and bathroom.

"This doesn't look like a prison," Ivy said.

"The windows and the door are enchanted," Thea said. "Unless one of my witches breaks the spell, you won't be able to leave this room."

Ivy nodded.

I knew this was coming, but I still hated to know she would be locked in this room. "It's temporary," I said. "Only until they know we can trust you."

Drake tilted his head. "Can we trust you?"

Ivy squared her shoulders and faced the witch queen. "You can. I know you won't, not for a long time, but I'm ready to wait for that."

"Well said." Thea nodded. "After Raika's call, I took the liberty to put some clean clothes in your closet and some toiletries in the bathroom. If the size is wrong, if you would like another style, or if anything is missing, let us know. I'll see to it personally."

"Thank you," Ivy muttered.

"You'll receive meals four times a day," Drake went on. "And I'll come back first thing in the morning to question you. The more you collaborate with us, the faster and easier this transition will be."

Ivy nodded. "Understood."

"Raika," Thea said. I turned to her. "You probably want to stay and we'll allow you to visit Ivy whenever you want, but Shane is almost here. Perhaps it would be a good idea for you to talk to him."

I frowned. She had said that as if they had a choice. Of course I would visit my sister! If they hadn't allowed it, I would have bought a fight. "Right." I looked at Ivy. "Are you okay? Do you need anything right now?"

She shook her head, a soft smile on her lips. "No, I'm good. I think I'll take a shower, put on clean clothes, and take a nap."

I nodded. "I'll come back later, then, okay?"

"Sure."

Thea and Drake walked out first, and with one last glance at Ivy, I exited the door. A vampire guard closed the door and the whoosh of magic ran over it.

Drake stared at me. "Raika, before Shane arrives, could we have a quick word with you in my office?"

Shit, I was in big trouble. "Yes."

I followed Drake and Thea to his office. Lavinia came with us, but the others dispersed—except for the handful of guards that stayed in front of the door, to make sure Ivy didn't break out.

In Drake's office, he gestured for us to take a seat. I sat down, and Lavinia sat in the chair beside mine. Thea took Drake's chair while he stood beside her.

"You know what we're going to say, right?" Thea asked.

I wanted to pout, but tried to keep my expression neutral. I felt like a kid who had messed up, got caught, and would now get a punishment by her parents—and Thea was only eight years older than me!

"I do," I said, my chin high. "That it was irresponsible, that I walked right into Paimon's trap, and he could have killed me, and then you wouldn't have a weapon."

Drake shook his head, but Thea was the one to speak, "Those things are true, but we weren't worried about you because you're the only who can stop Paimon. We were worried because of you, that simple."

"You're part of the DuMoir family now," Drake said. "We don't want to see any harm come to you."

That took me by surprise. I respected and liked them a lot, but we had met not long ago. I didn't expect them to care that much, and knowing they did warmed my heart.

"I'm sorry," I whispered. "It's just ... she's my sister, and I know she isn't evil. She has done bad things, yes, but it was because she was afraid of Paimon. He bullied her and she didn't know better. She thought that if she could please him, he would care more." So wrong. "But when she had to hurt me for him, she didn't. And when he tried hurting me, she stopped him."

"I remember how shocked you were," Lavinia said.

I nodded. "After that, Ivy tried leaving Paimon, but he locked her up. He wanted to use her as bait for me."

"Why you?" Drake asked.

"Because he wants my powers." Thea and Drake exchanged a worried look. "He wants the full dragon's magic, and he thinks that he can take it from me. Along with my darkfire. He wants it all."

"That will kill you," Thea muttered.

"I'm already dying," I reminded her. "But the thing is, if he gets my magic, he'll be unstoppable."

Drake narrowed his eyes at me. "Didn't he try to take it while you were there? How did you escape?"

I told him everything as best as I could. How I received Ivy's message, the inn, the portal, the cell, the waiting, the escape. "Unfortunately, he got the key back from me." That still hurt. If I had gotten the key, now we would have a huge advantage over her.

Drake's phone buzzed. He looked at it. "Shane is arriving. Before you go, there's one more thing we wanted to tell you."

Drake and Thea looked at Lavinia. I knew there was a reason she was here. I turned my body on my seat so I could face her.

"About eight months ago, maybe nine, I was kidnapped by the warlocks that had imprisoned Killian in another realm," she started. "They made me feed on dark magic and I lost myself. But no one here knew about it. The warlocks sent me back, pretending to be hurt. Then, in the middle of the night, I acted. I stole the boxes they needed, and I hurt vampires and witches before I left and went back to the warlocks." Her voice was full of grief. "I wasn't in control of myself. I didn't know what I was doing."

I nodded. "You're saying that Ivy could be like that right now."

Lavinia nodded. "I'm sorry, but that's why Drake and Thea want to keep her locked away for now. Until we know she has no spell or dark magic controlling her, and that she really wants to help, she'll remain in that room. I hope you understand."

My brows curled down. "I don't like it, but I understand." I saw their point. If Lavinia, the sweet-slash-badass girl in front of me could have turned against her friends without meaning to, then so could Ivy. Or anyone.

"All right." Thea pushed to her. "You should go now before Shane arrives and breaks down the castle searching for you."

One corner of my lips tugged up. "That sounds about right."

19

SHANE

THE FLIGHT BACK TO CONNECTICUT TOOK AN ETERNITY. I hadn't slept well the previous night during our first flight. We had fought a pack of wolves, and now I couldn't sleep because what Rotgar said seemed to be true.

Somehow, Paimon had lured Raika to him ... and she had gone to him?

No, she wasn't that stupid. There was an explanation to all of this. There had to be. I lay back on my seat, closed my eyes, and took a deep breath. Once more, I was glad the damn Shadow Wolf curse was gone, otherwise I would have already ripped this plane apart.

The moment the plane touched down and we could use our phones again, I got a text from Raika.

I'm back at the castle. I'll see you soon.

A mix of relief and frustration filled my chest. That was it? She wouldn't tell me what happened? I pressed the call button, but quickly turned it off. If I talked to her now, I would yell at her. Now that I knew she was back at the castle and safe, I could take time to calm down.

Yeah, right, as if I could.

We piled inside the SUVs and drove back to the castle. The ride was short, but my growing anxiety made it feel like it took hours.

Around four in the afternoon, Dom drove into the underground garage and steered the SUV to its spot.

Raika stood at the castle's entrance, as beautiful as ever.

My heart kicked hard and suddenly all of my apprehension and anger flew away.

The SUV hadn't even stopped when I jumped out, Dom yelling after me, and I ran to her.

Her bright, blue eyes rounded. "Shane, I—"

I slammed into her, wrapping my arms around her and holding her tight. I buried my face in her neck and inhaled deeply. She was here. She was fine. Whatever happened, whatever crazy thing she had done, it was the past. All that mattered was that she was back with me.

Her arms wound around my shoulders and she nestled her head on my chest. "I'm glad you're back and safe."

"I could say the same," I whispered in her hair.

"You're not going to yell at me?"

"I thought I would, but when I saw you standing there, my anger disappeared." Still holding her to me, I pulled my head back and looked at her pretty face. "I don't even care about what happened." What a lie. I cared, but I cared about her more.

"Hey, Raika," Dom said as he walked past us.

Lucille waved at Raika and said, "Hi girl," as she followed Dom inside the castle.

Killian gave Raika an army salute, and the other vampires nodded in greeting before all of them disappeared from the garage.

Raika let out a long sigh. "We should talk."

I frowned. I wasn't sure I wanted to talk just yet, but I knew we had to do it sooner rather than later. "Where do you want to go?"

She slipped her hand in mine. "How about we go for a walk?"

I nodded. Holding hands, we walked out the underground garage through the ramp, and found a stone path that wound through one of the castle's many gardens.

It was warm out, the sun still high and strong. The path was flanked by roses of many colors—red, pink, white, yellow … and their scent wafted through the air.

"Rotgar was there," I started. I hadn't planned on that, but the words came out. "He told me Paimon had sent him there so Serge could take over the Whitecrest pack."

She nodded. "I know. Paimon and Rotgar told me."

A heavy ball fell into my stomach and I halted on the path, making her stop. "So you fell for Paimon's trap."

"I fell for his trap on purpose." Then, she told me everything. Ivy's texts, meeting her at the inn, Paimon's trickery, spending the night with Ivy, getting the portal key, running away, losing the key. "Now Ivy is locked in a room in the castle as if she was a terrible criminal."

I nodded. I had held my breath for half of her narrative, battling against my anger and relief. When she told me Paimon had had her in his clutches, ready to take her power away, my heart wrenched in pain. Dear moon, this woman would give me a heart attack. "They are being cautious since something similar happened with Lavinia."

She frowned. "They told me about that. You were here back then, right?"

"Yes. We all thought we had rescued our friend, and she

was acting oddly because she had been kidnapped. But it had been a show to put us at ease. She didn't know what she was doing."

Raika nodded. "That's unfortunate. I know Ivy isn't like that, but I understand everyone's apprehension. I'm only okay with this because she's in a comfortable room and she'll be treated well."

"Our friends are fair."

"I know, and I know Ivy will prove to be useful. Soon, she'll be at our side, fighting against our enemies."

I bristled. "After we defeat Paimon, we could take a break from fighting for a while, don't you think?" I refused to think that a future with her was impossible unless we found a cure ASAP. Part of me wanted to run back to the library and continue researching until I found something, while the other wanted to stay right here with her. I wanted to stay by her side every second she had left.

She chuckled. "I agree. We could proclaim the Nightshade is on indefinite vacation and party all day long."

"That would be amazing." I stared at her, lost in her eyes, in her smile, in the wild hair, the shape of her neck, the curve of her breast.

A sudden rush of lust coursed through me. It was hard to contain myself whenever I was near her. It was a miracle I hadn't ravished her the moment I stepped out of the SUV.

I trailed my fingertips down her hair, her neck, her breast.

Raika's back arched, as if eager for my touch. "Shane," she whispered.

I lost it.

I claimed her mouth. Raika didn't hesitate. She opened her lips for me and clung to me as I pushed her away from the path and deeper into the garden. I pressed her against a thick tree, holding her captive.

She gasped when I broke the kiss and explored her neck with my teeth. Her hands skimmed down my arms, my stomach, and slipped inside the front of my pants. She cupped my hard-on and I groaned, biting her neck.

I brought my lips to her ear. "You have no idea how much I want you."

"Yes, yes, I do," she rasped. Her hand moved up and down my length, and I groaned again and pure pleasure spread through me. Dear moon, I had missed her, I had—

I stilled and moved away from her. "We can't. You'll lose control."

"I took two doses of the elixir, and I have an extra one right here," she said, her eyes practically pleading. "If you're afraid, that's okay. We can stop now, but if you trust me—"

I closed my mouth around hers, swallowing her words. I trusted her completely. Right now, I wanted her so bad.

Raika undid the zipper of my pants before continuing her game from before, moving her hand up and down my length, making me harder and harder. I moved my hips with her hand, as the ecstasy built up inside of me.

This woman ... the way her touch enticed me, the way the glint in her eyes made me content, the way her scent drove me crazy. She was everything to me.

I smoothed my hands down her arms, intent on taking her hands away, so we could continue this another way, but then I felt how hot her skin was.

I pulled back. "Raika, you're burning up."

"Shit." She took in a deep breath. "Yeah, I can feel it." She pouted. "I'm sorry."

"It's okay." I wanted to embrace her, to kiss her again, but I was afraid of what that could do to her, so I stood there, a foot from her and in deep agony. "Your health comes first."

She inhaled deeply a few more times then touched her forehead. "It's getting better."

I rested a hand on her arm. "Yes, it is, but we should stop bec—"

"I think there's something I can do, though." She knelt in front of me, tugged my pants down a little bit, and freed my hard-on. She closed her hand around it and I sucked in sharp breath.

"Raika," I growled.

"It's okay," she said, looking up at me. "This should be okay."

Then, she closed her mouth around me, and I cursed under my breath. I should tell her to stop, I should tell her she didn't need to do this, but damn, when it felt this good, I couldn't. Right now, I was at her mercy.

I was always at her mercy.

She licked my length, then closed her mouth around it, sucking it hard. She moved slow at first, but oh, so deep. After a few strokes, she sped up, taking me even deeper inside her mouth. Groaning, I slid my hands in her hair, cradling the back of her head. I couldn't help it. I moved my hips in rhythm with her, needing more, wanting more.

Desire and ecstasy coursed through me and I knew I wouldn't last. I groaned again. "Just keep going," I said, my voice thick.

To my surprise, Raika sped up.

Oh, shit.

My knees buckled, and I had to brace a hand on the tree behind Raika when I climaxed. I tried pulling away from Raika's mouth, but she gripped my ass and took everything in her mouth. When I stopped, she licked my length, making me shiver, and she smiled up at me.

"You ..." I growled.

She rose to her feet. "Me, what?"

Dear moon. I fisted her hair and pulled her to me. I kissed her so hard, I hoped to leave a permanent mark on her beautiful lips.

Mine, that was what it should say.

I broke the kiss, resting my forehead to hers. "That was ..." I took in a deep breath.

She smiled some more. "I'm glad you liked it."

It was a shame I couldn't pay her back. With a sigh, I zipped up my pants, made sure I looked presentable, then hand in hand, we strolled toward the village.

20

RAIKA

"This looks perfect, Chef Morris. Thank you." I kissed the old vampire's cheek. He smiled coyly at me and shooed me away from his kitchen. Clutching the heavy silver tray, I left and walked through the castle's hallways.

Last night, Shane and I had dinner in the village with Minsi, Tyren, Rue, Dom, and Lucille. Dom seemed a little off, and Shane said he had noticed Dom quieter since they came back from our pack lands.

"I'll talk to him," he promised.

After dinner, Shane and I came back to the castle. As much as I wanted to sleep in the house with the rest of our family, I knew that we couldn't predict everything. I had a lot more control over the dragon's magic, but it was still killing me, and one of these days, it would take over. Staying inside my bedroom, or near Thea and Almae, was the best solution right now.

This morning, Shane had left early to check on the pack —he would finally talk to Dom. He promised he would come back to the library after. I smiled at Chef Morris until he gave me a wonderful breakfast I could take to Ivy.

I was told she was served dinner last night and she had eaten it all. The food here was amazing, and she had been starved in the past few days.

I smiled at the tray in my hands. She would love breakfast.

The guards in front of her door saw me approaching and stepped aside. When one reached for the doorknob, the whoosh of the magic dropped, as if falling to the floor. He opened the door for me and I walked inside.

"Good morning ..." I looked around. "Ivy?"

"In here!" she called from the closet.

I placed the tray on the coffee table in front of the loveseat and stopped by the closet's entrance.

Wearing only underwear, Ivy held two dresses up. "This one or this one." I stared at them, confused. One was an indigo cocktail dress with a cinched waistline and a slight flare to its skirt. The other was an elegant black dress with square cuts.

"Hm, the dark blue will bring out your eyes."

"Right." She placed the black one back on the rack. She slipped the dress over her head. "How do I look?"

"Like you're going to a party."

She smiled at me. "Everyone in this place dresses up, like I used to do." She stared at my ripped shorts, tank top, and wedge boots. "Almost everyone." I rolled my eyes. "If I'm going to spend my day talking to vampires in suits and witches in pretty gowns, I don't want to feel underdressed."

"Of course." I sighed. "But let's talk about more important things. Are you hungry?"

Her eye lit up. "Famished."

I chuckled.

We sat down on the loveseat and Ivy dug in—Morris had made fresh sweet bread and muffins, an assorted fruit bowl, and we had plenty of drinks: coffee, orange juice, milk, and water.

With each bite, Ivy moaned. "This is divine."

"That was the same thing I said when I first tasted his food."

"Seriously, last night's dinner was steak that melted on my tongue, and steamed vegetables. It sounds so boring, but it was perfect. When I get out of here, I might buy this vampire out. I need him to cook every one of my meals."

For some reason, I was sure Morris couldn't be bought. "Good luck with that."

We ate the rest of our breakfast with small talk and laughter. When we were done, I pushed the tray aside and adjusted myself on the seat—one leg folded under me, my torso turned toward Ivy, my arm on the backrest.

"How did you sleep?"

Ivy's nose wrinkled. "Too many nightmares of Paimon destroying this castle and killing everyone in it to get to me and you."

"I'm sorry. Hopefully, these nightmares won't last long."

"Hopefully."

A knock came from the door and two seconds later, Lord Drake and Prince Cain walked into the room.

"I hope you had a good night," Drake said, walking toward us.

Ivy and I stood up. "I did. Thank you," Ivy said, adjusting her dress.

"Please sit down." Drake took one of the armchairs and

Prince Cain took the other. "If you don't mind, I would like to start our conversation."

"Of course." Ivy sat back down, her back straight as a rod.

I sat down, not even giving Drake a chance to send me away. I wanted to stay here and help Ivy with my support. It sounded silly, but I tried putting myself in her shoes and I thought I would like to have someone beside me who was in my corner.

"We don't have time to waste, so I'll get directly to the point," Drake said. "What do you know of Paimon's plan? What can you tell us that will give us an advantage over him?"

Ivy glanced at me, before fixing her eyes on the vampire lord. "Paimon has the key that opens the portal to the Huddyria realm."

"Huddyria?" Cain asked.

Ivy snorted. "I know, right? I had never heard of it before. But Huddyriuns are these incredibly strong and tall humanoids with weird skin and features. They are intelligent, but more brutal and rough than humans and other super-naturals."

"And these Huddyriuns are allowing him to use their realm?" Drake asked.

"There are several countries in Huddyria," Ivy said, making quotation marks with her fingers. "And within these countries, there are factions and sides. Paimon is paying one to allow him to use their place."

"Paying?" Cain asked. "Like money?"

Ivy shook her head. "No, they have no use for our money in their world. I don't know what Paimon is paying them with, but it certainly isn't good."

Drake and Cain exchanged a glance. "Continue," Drake said.

"Right." Ivy cleared her throat. "Hm, Paimon is keeping most of his army in Huddyria, so it's harder for you to find him, but he does have a couple of buildings and houses here and there, so he can hide whenever he's on Earth."

"Do you know the location of these buildings and houses?" Drake asked.

Ivy nodded. "Most of them, yes."

"Will you tell us?"

"Sure." She rattled off a handful of addresses, and Drake and Cain wrote those down in their phones.

After taking notes, Drake looked at Cain and Cain simply nodded. "I'm on it." The vampire prince got up and left the room.

My brow furrowed. I knew what that meant. Cain would arrange for groups of vampires to go to these places ASAP.

"Anything else?" Drake asked.

"Lord Drake, since he got the dragon's magic and I stopped him from hurting Raika, Paimon hasn't told me anything," Ivy said. "He's not stupid. Since yesterday, he must have changed his plans, because he knows I would tell you everything."

Drake nodded. "That's why we must act before he has a chance to regroup."

"His original plan was simple: get the dragon's magic, become the most powerful supernatural on Earth, and force his way back into the underworld and kill anyone who stood in his way. If the dragon's magic didn't do it, then he would kill another powerful supernatural and steal their powers. He had a list of names: you, Thea, Ariella, a warlock called Keeran, a coven of witches, and other supernaturals I had never heard of before. He would probably pick and choose whoever was easier to attack."

Drake's brows slammed down. "But he got only half of the dragon's magic."

"That's why he lured Raika to him," Ivy said. "But he underestimated her. I would say that by now, he has either already found and stolen the magic from another supernatural, or he's on his way to do so."

Drake typed on his phone, probably noting down all the names Ivy had said, and sending texts to these people, warning them. He stopped and looked at her. "Thank you, Ivy. I'll take care of a few things and I'll be back later."

She opened her arms wide. "I'm not going anywhere."

One corner of Drake's lips curled up. "See you later." He nodded at her and me, then spun on his heels and left the room.

The moment the door shut behind him, Ivy turned to me with wide eyes. "Are all vampires in this castle that hot? I mean, I only saw two, but holy hell, they are fine."

I chuckled. "You saw more vampires yesterday when you arrived."

Ivy waved me off. "I was too distressed yesterday to look at them."

"Well, Lord Drake and Prince Cain are taken," I told her. "They have soulmates, so hold your horses."

Ivy shook her head. "What a shame."

I smiled. "Glad to see you're still the same Ivy."

"Hm, my pride is a little wounded, and I'm a little ashamed for taking this long to realize Paimon was using me, manipulating me, that he never cared and never will."

I reached over and placed my hand on hers. "Forget about him. You have me now and I care."

She smiled back at me. "I might have lied to you that we were best friends, though I had a feeling that would have been true if we had grown up together."

"I had the same feeling," I told her.

UNFORTUNATELY, I COULDN'T SPEND THE ENTIRE DAY WITH IVY because I had to train with Thea. Since Thea knew I would spend a good part of the morning with Ivy, we had agreed to meet later, and I still had to rush to get to the clearing on time.

"Sorry, I'm late," I said, panting.

"Only ..." Thea glanced at her the screen of her phone. "Seven minutes. It's fine and understandable. If I suddenly found out I had a sister and had brought her back into my life, I'm not even sure I would have come to training."

One corner of my lips tugged up. "I thought about canceling, but I know this is important." If not more important, at least right now. Until we defeated Paimon, none of us would be free and safe from him.

"Wise words," Thea said. "Let's start so you can go back to Ivy."

I liked that.

As usual, my first spell was to conjure both the darkfire and the dragon's magic as fast as I could and simultaneously. The two magics still warred inside me, wanting full control, but not like before. Now, it was almost like a faint scream in the back of my mind. I barely noticed it anymore.

Next, I played with both magics, shaping them as I wanted, throwing them here and there, then at targets Thea created with her magic. Then at moving targets.

Two hours in, I had an idea.

Thea conjured five blue figures spread out through the clearing. Instead of attacking them immediately, I closed my eyes and focused. I half expected Thea to ask me what was going on, but she knew I was up to something and she would wait to see what it was.

Inspired by her magic, I first conjured a figure made of darkfire in front of one of Thea's. Then, I conjured one made of dragon's magic.

Next, I conjured one made of both.

This time, the magics fought harder against each other. My teeth gritted as I commanded them into submission. I opened my eyes as the shape took form, the two magics intertwining in every limb. My arms shook with the effort to hold on to the figure.

My mixed-up soldier stood for whole eight seconds before it fizzled into bright smoke. The other two figures followed suit.

I fell to my knees, panting.

Thea smiled at me. "That was unexpected and incredible."

I gestured to where my failed soldiers had stood. "It didn't work."

"But it did. You might not be able to hold on to them yet, but you were able to make them. That's a big step." She offered me a hand, helping me up. "Remember when you couldn't even conjure both magics together and now ... look at you!"

I tilted my head. "When you put it that way."

She chuckled. "Come on. You deserve a break." We walked to the edge of the clearing, where she had left a bag with water and snacks under the shade of a tree.

I grabbed a water bottle and drank half of it in one gulp. It was getting hotter and hotter, something I wasn't used to. Until a few months ago, I had lived in a protected place, where it never got too hot or too cold.

Thea leaned against the tree, checking her phone.

"Any news from the raid?" I asked her. Right after our conversation, Prince Cain had left with a big group of vampires to check the buildings and houses Ivy had told him and Drake about. Ivy told them which ones were decoys, and the ones served to house demons and weapons when they were on Earth.

Thea lowered her phone and shook her head. "Too many places to check."

Her phone rang. She glanced at the screen and frowned. "Hey," she answered.

Thanks to my wolf hearing, I heard as Drake said, "We failed."

21

SHANE

"SHE'S WHAT?"

Dom rolled his eyes. "My mate, man. Anne is my mate."

It sounded like a bad joke, but it wasn't.

When I left the castle early this morning, I called Dom first thing. He had been acting weird since the fight at Nightshade yesterday and when I asked him what happened, he had evaded me. This morning, I gave him no choice. If he didn't tell me, I would use my alpha's command and make him tell me.

The last thing I expected him to tell me was that during the fight, he grappled with a female wolf from the Ironfang pack and the mating bond snapped. They didn't even have a chance to talk about it.

"Why didn't you tell me?" I asked. "I would have given you more time."

Dom shook his head. "No, you wouldn't. Raika was missing and you wouldn't wait a single second to come back here."

Right. "Then I would have left you there and you would have come back later."

Dom leaned against the wall of my office in our town hall. He crossed his arms. "I was too shocked to do anything. One moment, we were fighting for our lives and the bond snapped, the next moment, we were leaving."

I frowned. "Did you get her number? Have you talked to her since then?"

Dom looked down. "No, there was no time. I barely learned her name before we left." He pressed a hand on his chest. "Leaving her behind fucking hurt. It still does."

I knew how that felt. "It won't stop hurting until you're with her. Like physically close."

"Shit," he muttered.

"Call Eike," I told him. Dom had his number. "He's her alpha now. Ask him to give you her number. Talk to her. Invite her to come here." His eyes hardened. "You are mates, Dom. You're meant to be together."

"I know that, but maybe now that things are peaceful over there, I shouldn't ask her to come here, to where the threat of a battle is hanging over our heads."

One corner of my lips tugged up. His protective instinct was strong. "Then don't invite her to come yet, but talk to her. She's probably as shocked as you are."

He gave me a side glance. "Who are you and what have you done with my brutish, dumb best friend?"

I chuckled. "One, I was never dumb. Two, I'm only brute when the occasion calls for it. Three, I'm mated, man. I know how that feels, and all I wish for you is to be with your mate."

"Mate? Someone said mate?" Lucille walked into my office. Her eyes widened as she looked at a brooding Dom. "You have a mate? Who?"

He grunted, but told her about Anne.

"Ah, I can't wait to meet her." Then her lips pouted. "What about me, huh? No mates for me? I'll be the crazy aunt to all your kids? Ugh."

"Well—" I was going to joke she could be mated to Tyren, who had been smitten with her for a while now, but my phone rang. I picked it up and straightened in my chair upon seeing the name on the screen. "Kaz."

"Hi, Shane, sorry for only getting back to you now. I was away, with no cell reception."

He was probably in that secretive place, where his race and the dragons lived. "I understand."

"What happened? Is there anything I can help you with?"

"It's Raika ..." I told him she now had more control of the dragon's magic, but the witches determined the magic was killing her. We had been researching like crazy, but so far, we hadn't found anything promising. "I thought ... maybe you know something they don't and could help Raika. Save her." I held my breath.

"The magic she has is stolen," Kaz said with a bitter tone. He was still upset about what happened that day. "There's nothing we can do to stop it from killing her." I ran a hand over my face. "But ... I can go there if you want. I can take a look at her, see if there's anything I can do to ease her pain."

Currently, she was not in pain, but I wouldn't deny the help of a dragon shifter. "Sure. Please. Come."

I told him where to find the castle, and Kaz assured me he would be here tomorrow morning. We turned off the call, and despite him telling me he didn't know how to help her, I felt a waft of hope dancing around my chest.

"That is good, right?" Lucille asked. "Maybe he can do something for her."

Dom nodded. "Maybe he'll examine her, determine it's not as bad as the witches think, and he'll be able to cure her."

I inhaled deeply, holding on to the hope in me. "He has to be able to do something."

My phone rang again, this time it was Killian. I answered and he said, "Come to the castle for a meeting."

DOM AND I MADE OUR WAY TO THE CASTLE. LUCILLE WANTED to come, mostly out of curiosity, but since she wasn't my beta, she couldn't. I had invited Tyren. He was playing video games at Hugh's house, but dropped it and met Dom and me halfway to the castle.

We arrived at the conference room beside Drake's office, and I greeted everyone: Raika, Thea, Almae, Lavinia, Killian, Dorian, and Aston.

I went to Raika, settling in a chair beside her. Tyren sat next to me, and Dom sat on Tyren's other side.

"What's going on?" I asked Raika in a whisper.

"Lord Drake is—" She stopped and jutted her chin to the door. Drake walked into the room and everyone stopped talking.

He walked to the head of the table, but didn't sit down. He looked at us, his eyes grave. "Ivy's intel was good. The buildings and houses she told us about belong to Paimon, though most of them had been emptied by the time Prince Cain and his men arrived."

"Most?" Killian asked.

Drake nodded. "There was one building Ivy said was housing most of the demons. It was clear they were evacuating when Cain arrived, but they were prepared."

"What do you mean?" Almae asked.

"Cain and his men killed at least a dozen demons and emptied the place, but we lost two vampires in the fight," Drake said, his voice grave.

Tension built in the air.

"But these buildings and houses are secured now, right?" Almae asked. "Paimon can't use them anymore?"

Drake nodded. "Elisa and Zadkiel went with Prince Cain. She spelled the locations so if any demons try to enter it, a spell will hold them in place and we'll receive an alert."

Many heads nodded, mine included. That was a good plan.

"But there's more," Drake said. Everyone stilled. "I received word from Hadrian. Paimon and his demons attacked another underworld gate this morning."

"What?" I asked.

Drake sighed. "No one was expecting it after what happened yesterday ..." We all glanced at Raika. "But that was precisely why he did it. Now that Ivy is with us and telling us all of his plans, he's changing everything."

"Or she's lying," Prince Dorian said.

Raika stiffened. "She's not lying."

Dorian lifted both hands. "I'm bringing the possibility to the table."

I frowned. Killian had told me Dorian could be a jerk sometimes, and he liked to instigate mistrust and doubt. Lord Drake kept him as a prince, and Killian said that even though Dorian could be a prick, he was also an incredibly good fighter, and sometimes, his absurd ideas and suggestions were right.

"I've thought about that," Drake said. "That's why this

morning I asked Morris to put a few drops of a truth elixir in her food before our conversation."

Raika's eyes widened. "You didn't trust her."

"It takes a lot for me to trust someone," Drake said. "I couldn't risk everyone in this castle for a demon who could be lying to us. What if she fed us wrong information and send us into a trap? It happened before."

I glanced from him to Lavinia. It had been different, but Lavinia had also been allowed back after being with our enemies, and when we least expected it, she attacked us.

I understood Drake's point.

From the way Raika's shoulders drooped, I knew she did too. "I think she would have told you the truth even without the elixir."

"She did," Thea said. "I made the elixir so that if the person tries to lie and the elixir forces the truth out, with a high-pitched voice the person can't control. But nothing happened. Ivy told us the truth."

Dorian humphed.

"What happened to the gate?" I asked. If Paimon was in the underworld, no one would be seated calmly here, right?

"Paimon opened a portal right in front of the gate, as he did last time," Drake said. "Though this time, his demons came through."

"And the coward?" Killian asked.

Drake nodded. "He came too. But the demon hunters' response was swift. Hadrian, Rey, and Erin fought Paimon and pushed him back." Drake glanced at Raika. "He was too strong for the three of them, and as much as they tried, they couldn't kill him."

Raika inhaled. "Only I can."

"We still think so, yes," Drake said. "But we won't know for sure until you face him."

My gut knotted. I loathed the idea of Raika standing before her father again, but what other choice did we have?

Raika looked at Thea. "We should go back to training."

"No more training," Dorian snapped. "How many demon hunters did his demons kill earlier today? Too many, I bet." Drake nodded. He probably knew the exact number. "We need to act now. We can't wait for his next move."

"We need a plan," Drake said. "I'll be meeting with Hadrian, Rey, and Erin later this afternoon along with a few others. We won't leave this meeting until we have a solid plan we can put into action ASAP." He looked around the room. "Anything else before I dismiss you all?"

I nodded. "Yes." All eyes turned to me. "I talked to Kaz. He's coming here to help with Raika and the dragon magic."

Raika's eyes bugged. "He has a cure?"

I shook my head. "No, but he wants to examine you and help you with your training, I think."

Her chest deflated.

"That's good," Drake said. "Any help is welcomed." He looked at all of us again. "I'm leaving for the meeting. In the meantime, be prepared. We might face Paimon again at any time."

Drake extended his hand to Thea. She took it, got up, and the two of them left the room together. Prince Dorian and Prince Aston were next.

Killian and Lavinia stayed. They leaned over the long table, looking at us.

"Kaz is coming, then?" Killian asked.

I nodded. "He'll arrive tomorrow morning."

22

RAIKA

I didn't sleep well.

There was too much going on for me to relax—Ivy was locked in a room, Drake was still in his meeting with the demon hunters, Paimon had boldly attacked a gate, but failed, and Kaz was arriving to check on me.

Besides, Shane slept shirtless beside me and my thoughts drifted to his glorious physique, and my body kept heating up. I had to drink an elixir, take a cold shower, and just sit away from him before I exploded again.

Early morning, Shane and I took breakfast to Ivy. It was time he met her while they were not trying to kill each other. At first, they were both tense around each other, but slowly, they got comfortable.

My heart warmed watching them both. My mate and my sister.

Kaz sent a text to Shane when he was entering the DuMoir estate. Shane and I said goodbye to Ivy—I promised to visit her later—and we headed to the castle's front doors.

The sound of a bike reached my ears before I could see it

in the distance. A fancy Harley Davidson rolled down the road, stopping before the stone staircase.

Kaz took off his helmet and hopped off his bike.

Shane and I walked down the stairs to greet him.

"Kaz." Shane grabbed Kaz's forearm and they shook arms like that. "Thanks for coming."

Kaz appraised me with his dark green eyes, a knot between his brows. "How are you feeling?"

Was it me, or had he grown more stoic and brooding since the last time I saw him? Well, that wasn't saying much. The last time I saw him, he was badly hurt and he was pissed at me for having accidentally received half of the dragon's magic.

"Right now, okay." But that was because I had taken the elixir not long ago.

"We don't have time to waste," he said. He lifted the seat of his bike and grabbed a small duffel bag from it. "Let me examine you and let's see what I can do for you."

"Of course." I gestured for him to follow us. "Please, come this way."

Kaz followed us through the castle's hallways. Something about the way he took in everything told me he was a trained warrior and he was now doing inventory of any threats or emergency exits.

We arrived at the infirmary where Thea, Almae, and Meredith waited for us. Lavinia wanted to come too, but she decided against it. "It'll be a crowd in there," she said.

"It's nice to meet you, Kaz," Thea said with a polite smile.

Kaz grunted and nodded at her. Then he turned to me. He grabbed my elbow and steered me to the center of the room. "Just stand still and let me do my thing."

Shane took two steps back, though I could see the tension in his body, but hope shone from his dark eyes.

As for me, I had no hope. I couldn't deal with hope right now.

Kaz's eyes turned amber, and scales covered his bare arms. He walked around me, not even touching me, or hovering his hands over me. He just looked at me with those weird eyes.

After what felt like an eternity—it was probably less than fifteen minutes—Kaz's eyes and arms returned to normal. He halted right in front of me, his brows furrowed.

"So?" I asked, realizing there was a little hope in my voice. Shit.

"I have to say, I've never seen anything like this."

"What does that mean?" Shane asked.

Kaz let out a grunt. "It's not good. The witches are right. The magic attached to you in such a way that would be impossible to pull it out without killing you. And yet, you're dying because the magic needs too much and your body isn't strong enough."

"What body would be strong enough?" Almae asked.

"None."

"But dragon shifters?" Thea asked. "Aren't they—?"

"There was only one human who became a dragon shifter," I said, interrupting Thea without meaning to. The words needed to come out. "Alice. The dragon chose her and performed a ritual to bind her to her powers. Without it, she wouldn't survive."

Kaz nodded, the glint in his eyes amused.

"What if another dragon performed the ritual?" Almae asked.

"They can't," I answered again. "It has to be the dragon who willingly gives his magic." And that dragon was dead.

Kaz grunted. "Correct."

"So there's nothing you can do for her?" Shane asked.

Kaz picked up a leather pouch from his bag and handed it to me. "Take these."

I grabbed the pouch, opened it, and spied inside. I picked up one of the small candy-sized white tablets. "What's this?"

"Medicine from my elders," Kaz said. "It should help you with any pain you have, and also slow down the dragon's magic." He lifted a finger. "It won't stop it, though. You'll just have more time."

"How long?" I asked, my voice low.

Kaz shook his head. "A week more? A month? It's not something I can predict."

I would take it. If it gave me a day more, I would take it. I shoved the tablet in my mouth and swallowed. A bitter taste filled my mouth, but nothing I couldn't deal with. Meredith handed me a glass of water and I thanked her for it.

"Kaz," I said as a new thought came to mind. "Paimon, the former underworld prince who got the other half of the magic. He told me he's not experiencing anything. He has not lost control, or almost exploded, or anything of the like. Is that possible?"

Kaz frowned. "I don't know. He was one of the most powerful supernaturals in the world until a couple of years ago, wasn't he?"

I nodded.

"I never heard of a demon with dragon shifter, or a dragon shifter who mated with a demon, so I have no idea what would happen. I can only guess he either lied to you, or depending on how strong the supernatural is, he really is fine. That would be a new development and I'm certain my elders would like to hear about it."

I considered this. Had he lied to me? Why? So I wouldn't think he was weak? And if he was having the same trouble as I was, why was he so keen on having the rest of the dragon magic? To die faster? Unless, he had found a way of curing it. Or he thought that once he had the full power, he would be okay?

There was too much to unpack here.

Thea rested a hand on my arm. "This doesn't change anything. We shouldn't waste the day away. Let's go train."

I nodded.

"I'll train her today," Kaz said.

THEA WENT AHEAD WITH KAZ AND ALMAE, WHILE I WALKED with Shane to the library. Once more, he would spend some time there, looking for answers he wouldn't find, but who was I to stop him? If our roles were reversed, I would do the same thing.

Hand in hand, we halted outside the library's entrance. For some reason, after hearing Kaz say he couldn't help me, it had become real. I was dying and I would leave this handsome man alone.

I stepped into him, resting my cheek on his chest. His strong arms wound around me and his chin rested on top of my head.

"Are you okay?" he whispered.

"No, yes, maybe?" I sighed. "We should invite our friends for dinner tonight. Can we grill hamburgers and hot dogs in the backyard? That would be cool."

"Shouldn't you stay at the castle?"

"Perhaps, but I can drink the elixir and take Kaz's tablet right before we go. Plus, we can invite Kaz. If I start feeling like I'll explode, he can fly me away from there in seconds. With his dragon scales, he's probably impervious to fire, so I wouldn't hurt him." I hoped. "And, if you're worried, I can ask Thea to draw a witch's circle in the backyard. If anything goes wrong, you all step outside."

"That shouldn't be necessary." Shane's arms tightened around me. "Let's do it. I'll text everyone." He kissed the top of my head. "Now go before they come hunting you down."

I pulled back, arching an eyebrow at him. "Are you trying to get rid of me?"

He snorted. "Right. As if that was a thing." He pointed to the long table inside the library, with tall piles of books. "Those books won't read themselves."

I groaned. "This is a switch. You should go train, and I should read."

With a small smile, Shane leaned into me, pressing his lips to mine. "Now go before I hold on to you for real."

I loved hearing that because I knew it was true. I stood on my tiptoes, pressed another kiss to his mouth, then sauntered away. After a handful of steps, I looked back and Shane stood there, looking at me with a smile on his lips and a happy glint in his eyes.

That made me happy.

I turned a corner and went down the stairs.

Prince Dorian was walking up the stairs with two of his vampires. "Drake isn't back yet?" he asked one of the vampires.

"No, my prince."

Dorian cursed under his breath. "This meeting has been

going for too long."

My feet halted and I stared at the prince. "Wait. Are you saying Lord Drake is still out? For the same meeting he left for yesterday?"

The prince frowned at me. I was well aware he didn't like many people but I didn't care.

"The demon hunters needed sleep so he came back late at night," he said, his tone sharp, as if he wasn't happy about telling me this. "But he left again early this morning and from the latest report—" He gestured to his vampire. "—the meeting has reached no conclusion and will continue indefinitely. Now, if you'll excuse me." He turned his back to me and continued up the stairs, his two vampires following him.

I stood in place, shocked. They were still talking about how to defeat Paimon? There had to be something they could do, some advantage they had over my father, some strategy they could use.

Oh, I knew what. Something I had thought of before and something that I knew would work.

"Wait." I raced after Prince Dorian.

He slowed at the top of the stairs but didn't stop. "What is it now?"

I stepped in front of him and he halted. "I need to talk to Lord Drake. And to Hadrian, Rey, Erin, and whoever else is at this meeting."

The prince's brows curled down. "Are you insane, girl? You were allowed in a couple of meetings, but most of them are for top-ranked officials. Not even I was invit—"

"Please. I promise you, they need to hear me."

Dorian appraised me. He knew I was important to this battle. I was the one who had to kill Paimon, wasn't I? He couldn't deny me this.

"Fine," he groaned. "Come with me."

PRINCE DORIAN TOOK ME TO ONE OF THE CASTLE'S courtyards. He called someone, talking in hushed tones that even I couldn't hear, then hung up. A few seconds later, a portal opened up and Aspen stepped through it.

He offered me his hand. "I'll take you to Lord Drake."

I glanced from his hand to Dorian. He wasn't messing with me here, right? No, Aspen had taken us before to and from one of the underworld gates.

I slipped my hand in his, allowing him to pull me through the portal.

We arrived at the Winnipeg gate and a buzz of activity and people surrounded us. It was colder here and heavy, dark thunderclouds covered the sky.

Aspen pointed to the tent. "They are in there."

I frowned. He wasn't going to escort me there? As long as I got my message to them, I didn't care how it was delivered.

I walked to the tent. When I was a few feet from it, I could make out the figures inside, and Lord Drake, who stood in front of the desk, saw me coming.

I walked inside the tent and lowered my head a little. "Sorry for the interruption, but—"

Drake frowned. "Prince Dorian told me you were coming with an important message. What is it?"

I looked around the table—Hadrian, Rey, and Erin were here along with Keeran, Luana, Ariella, Wyatt, Farrah, and a couple of others I didn't know.

I cleared my throat and lifted my chin. "I have a plan to draw Paimon out."

23

SHANE

I RESEARCHED FOR A COUPLE OF HOURS—AND BECAME increasingly frustrated with the lack of answers. I talked to Elisa, who had been supervising research at the Silverblood estate and the Silver Moon Academy, and she said they had found nothing.

"I have also reached out to other covens," she said. "And last night they sent reports with the same."

Though I expected that, a pang cut through my core at the news.

I wanted to spy on Raika's training with Kaz, but I decided to be a good partner and organize the barbecue she had asked for. I had been the one grilling her about spending more time with family, hadn't I? Now I had to deliver.

I went back to the village, checked on a few things at the town hall, and made sure all the big problems were either solved or being dealt with. I texted Dom and Lucille and asked them to make sure we had all the supplies—patties, wieners, buns, drinks, and whatnot.

At the house, I took a shower, put on dark jeans and a green Henley, and then greeted Minsi and Rue as they arrived.

"I thought this was a barbecue," Rue teased me. I had sent her and the others a text officially inviting them for dinner. "Not a ball."

I groaned. "A ball? Seriously?" I wasn't even wearing slacks or a polo shirt!

She chuckled, glad to rile me up.

Quiet as ever, Minsi went to her bedroom, picked up a pile of books, and then set them beside a chair on the back porch. Well, at least she would be around us. I made a mental note to invite her to dance with me at least once later tonight.

Tyren arrived with Hugh and the two of them promptly plopped down on Tyren's bed and started playing video games. "Call me when the party starts," Tyren said absently, twisting the controller in his hand as his fingers deftly worked the buttons.

I stared at Rue. Seriously? This was my beta? This was what I got for recruiting a fifteen-year-old. With time, I knew it would be better. He needed to learn to be a better alpha than I was.

Dom and Lucille came over with lots of bags. Rue and I helped them preparing the buns, the hot dogs, plastic plates and cups, and the drinks.

Not long after, Killian and Lavinia showed up. I asked about Raika, but Lavinia said she wasn't back from practice yet. I glanced at the clock—it read seven in the evening—and then out the window. The sun still hadn't disappeared behind the trees.

It was okay; there was no reason to panic.

Raika was with Thea, Almae, and Kaz. They were all capable and powerful.

Still, apprehension built up inside. She never trained this late. Was this because she had started late?

We took everything outside. Lucille put on some music on her phone and hooked it up to wireless speakers she had brought over from her house. Dom prepared the grill and nursed a beer, a constant scowl on his face now.

"Have you talked to Anne?" I asked.

He shook his head. "I got her number from Eike, but she didn't answer my calls or reply to my texts." He grunted. "I'm going insane. Isn't she? Doesn't she feel the same?"

I frowned. She should feel the same, but some people were better at self-control than others. "I bet this is hard for her too."

"What about this is hard? She's my mate. She should be with me."

"Dom, you live thousands of miles away, at least for now, and she probably has family and responsibilities," Lucille said, joining the conversation. "And she now has a new alpha and her pack doubled in size. I bet everything is a mess there and she can't deal with it all at the same time." She grabbed a beer from the cooler. "I want to find my mate, but if he lives too far away and shit is still blowing up around us, I don't know. I'm not changing anything about me, my ways, and my home to please my mate."

It was good to hear her say that because until a few months ago, she had tried changing several times, thinking I would take her back. I was glad she had moved on and was now waiting for something better. I hoped her mate was a good guy.

Finally, Raika arrived with Thea, Almae, and Kaz.

"I asked Thea and Almae to come draw the circle," she told me. "Just to be safe."

After they were done, we invited them to stay, but they said they had lots to prepare for the battle that was coming. Kaz stayed. He grabbed a beer, and sat down on one of the porch chairs near Minsi. She froze at first, but when he found some paper and pencil and began drawing beautiful dragons in detail, he won her over. The guy was an artist.

"Who knew the dragon shifter could draw?" Dom asked, sounding amused.

"And he came on an expensive-looking Harley Davidson," Raika said.

Lucille's eyes rounded. "Can a wolf shifter have dragon shifters as mates? Because he's a fine specimen and I wouldn't be opposed to that."

Raika chuckled. "You reminded me of Ivy. When she first met Kaz, all she talked about was getting into his pants."

"Ivy has good taste." Lucille winked.

I groaned. "Can we change the subject?"

"What I can do is raise the volume so we can have a real party." Lucille found her phone and speakers and messed with them.

"I thought this was a family-slash-friends dinner," Dom mused.

"A family dinner party," Lucille said over the music.

A slow ballad started and I glanced at Minsi. She was quiet, an open book in her lap, her eyes glued to Kaz and his drawings. I had promised myself I would dance with her, but now didn't seem like a good time.

So, I took another person.

When I tugged Raika to the middle of the backyard, she didn't resist one bit. She wrapped her arms around my neck and let me guide her as we swayed side to side. I wasn't a great dancer, but this was an excuse to be with her. It felt freaking great to have her in my arms.

"Did I tell you I love you?" I asked. Raika tilted her head, pretending to think. "Today, I mean."

A smile spread over her kissable lips. "I don't think so. But go ahead. I won't stop you."

I huffed. "You smartass." She winked at me. Holy moon ... I leaned into her and brushed my lips on hers. She inhaled deeply and moved even closer to me when I pulled back. I stared at her. "I love you."

"I love you too."

I kissed her again, and it was so damn hard to keep it family friendly. I had to force myself to stop before I dragged her inside the house. She was getting better at controlling the dragon magic, but we shouldn't risk it, not when so close to our family and friends.

After another song, I noticed Kaz had gone to the food table and Minsi was alone on the porch. Taking advantage of that opportunity, I excused myself from Raika and asked Minsi to dance with me. At first, she didn't want to, so I sat down beside her. I stayed there, doing nothing. A few minutes later, I asked, and again she said no.

Then Raika danced with Tyren.

"Look, Raika and Tyren," I said, my voice gentle. "Want to join them?"

Minsi hesitated, but finally, she nodded.

The next three hours flew by.

Until everyone started cleaning up then leaving, and it

was the five of us—Minsi, Tyren, Rue, Raika, and me. Rue would stay with the kids because Raika and I needed to go back to the castle.

We sat down on the living room couch with the kids, and even though I knew Raika wanted to do this, I felt like running away. Rue, also not wanting to hear it again, occupied herself in the kitchen.

"I have something to tell you," Raika started.

I almost clamped my ears.

Tyren frowned. "You're sick?"

Raika looked at me and I let out a long sigh. She continued, "It's more than that. The dragon magic is draining my energy and literally consuming me."

Tyren went rigid. "What does that mean?"

Tears sprang to Raika's eyes. "I'm dying."

Tyren shook his head vehemently, his hands closed into fists.

Minsi went pale. She opened her mouth in a big O, but no sound came out.

Raika reached for Minsi. "Breathe, pretty girl. You need to breathe." She breathed in and out, but Minsi didn't do it with her.

Instead, she screamed.

This time, I clamped my ears. But only for two seconds. Then I rushed to her and embraced her tightly. "I'm here," I whispered in ear. "I'm here for you. I won't let you go through his alone."

Then Raika's arm went around Minsi and me, and then Tyren's.

"I'm sorry about this," Raika whispered, her voice breaking.

Minsi started wailing, but Raika averted what seemed the

beginning of a panic attack. She lay down in Minsi's bed with her, while Tyren and I sat on the floor beside the bed. With tears in her eyes, Rue appeared by the door and watched over us.

At least for now, we were all together.

24

RAIKA

It took a while, but Shane and I went back to the castle. We were quiet on the way, each of us lost in our own thoughts—and I planned on something.

As soon as we entered our suite, I pressed his chest until he was seated at the edge of the bed.

"What's going on?" he asked.

"Just ... stay here. I'll be right back.

I ran into the closet and changed; I hadn't planned on this until a few minutes ago, but now that it was on my mind, I couldn't ignore it. This could be one of my last nights with Shane. I wanted it to be special.

After changing, I drank the elixir and took one of the tablets—this should help.

I walked out of the closet, wearing a black silk robe that went down to my knees.

Shane frowned. "Oh-kay."

I sat down beside him, feeling good, bold, and naughty. "Shane, I want you to make love to me."

His eyes rounded. "But—"

"Not buts." I scooted closer to him, until my knees touched his. "Just go with it."

Sucking a sharp breath, Shane slid his hand up my legs. I leaned back on the bed and he came with me, crawling over me. He pressed his body down on mine and his mouth to mine. I parted my lips and let him in. Kissing him was just too good, too hot. His taste, his tongue, the way his lips fit mine ... so perfect.

He glided his hands under my robe, but then I broke the kiss and pushed him away.

"What the ...?"

"Relax." I stood, a wicked smiled on my lips. "Relax and enjoy." I untied the robe and let it fall down to the floor, revealing red lace lingerie.

His mouth fell open. "By the moon ..."

His eyes skimmed over me, as if he didn't know where to look first.

"Do you like it?" I asked.

He cocked an eyebrow. "Is that a trick question?"

He reached for me but I slapped his hands away. "I'm in charge here."

Rolling with the high, I placed my hand on Shane's shoulders, pushed him down on the bed, and straddled him. His eyes went wide and his mouth parted, but his amused shock didn't stop his hands from closing around my waist. I adjusted myself, pressing my pelvis against his, all the while staring into his eyes, loving how the surprise in them morphed into lust.

"Raika," Shane whispered, a line of worry etched on his forehead. "Are you sure about this?"

"I'm sure. Trust me."

"Oh, I trust you."

Running my hands over his taut biceps, I leaned into him and brushed my lips on his. So soft, so warm. His eyes fluttered close, and he groaned. He slid one of his hands up my back and clasped my nape, holding me close. Then, he crashed his mouth against mine, claiming my every breath. His soft lips moved in a sensual, almost frantic rhythm, and his tongue provoked mine, making me moan. His hand on my waist snaked to the small of my back, pressing my breasts against his chest.

Drowning in desire, I rolled my hips, increasing the friction between us. He broke the kiss and drew in a sharp breath.

I took advantage of that pause to tug his shirt up. He helped me take it off, and then his hands were around my back, pulling me to him. His mouth found my neck. He grazed his tongue on my skin, making me shiver. Eager to touch him, to taste him, I bent closer, reaching for him, but he grasped my upper arms and held me back.

"Hey, I'm in charge," I complained.

"A pause in the game," Shane said. "I just ... need to look at you for a second." His husky, thick voice wrapped around me, drawing another shiver from me. I was self-conscious and excited by the way his gaze skimmed my body. It was as if he was devouring every inch of me with his eyes. His fingertips traced the cup of my bra from the middle of my chest, up the strand to my shoulder. That simple, fluttering touch ignited my skin, sending waves of want to all my nerve endings, and I shivered again.

I loved the way he looked at me.

"You're hot, perfect," he said. The corners of his lips curled up as he reached behind me and undid the clasp of my lingerie. He drew in a breath as his eyes scanned my body. "Fuck, Raika, you're beautiful."

Finally, Shane reached for me, hooking an arm around my waist and clasping one of my breasts with his free hand. He lowered his face to my chest and fitted his mouth on my other breast. His tongue lapped one nipple while he pinched the other, making me cry out. Heat rushed through my body, settling between my thighs.

Then, the hand on my breast slid down. Down my lingerie skirt and in between my thighs. He rubbed his hand on my entrance, making me hiss, before slipping a finger inside me. I cried out, but he didn't stop. He didn't relent. He kept sucking on my breast and pumping hard inside me. One, then two fingers. Then, as if that wasn't enough, he used his thumb to graze my clit. God, I was a goner.

I felt the heat surging up, the dragon's magic waking up, but I shoved it aside with all I had left. It wouldn't take this from me. Not now.

Shane pushed in once more, timing it perfectly with his tongue on my nipple and his thumb on my clit, and I was done for. The climax hit me hard and I trembled in his arms.

I hadn't burst into flames! I wanted to celebrate, but I didn't want to waste time. I didn't know how long the effects of the medicine and my self-control would last.

However, Shane was making me crazy, so I would make him crazy too.

Still trembling, I moved over and tugged his pants down. I threw them aside, then I sat over him again. I reached between my legs, pulled the skirt to the side, then slid him inside me. Very slowly. Shane groaned, and I sucked in a sharp breath.

I started moving, up and down, up and down. Shane tensed and cursed and tensed some more, while I took him as deep as I could. The friction was too much, too good. But I wanted more. I wanted all of him. As if reading my thoughts, Shane slid down the bed a little more and lifted his hips, changing the angle and letting me take him even deeper. I cried out as I pumped up and down, up and down, almost frenzied.

The heat consumed and I felt my walls tightening. Another climax was close, and I wanted it.

"Not yet," Shane whispered. He wrapped his arm around my waist and stood, carrying me with him. He deposited me over the round table on the other side of the room. "I've been wanting to try this with you for a long time."

He thrust into me hard and deep, taking me to heights I didn't think existed. All I could do was ask for more, more, more, as I felt my climax closing in again.

"Damn, you feel so good." Shane gave me more. Holding my waist, he pulled me faster, harder, deeper.

"Oh ..." Pleasure exploded inside me and I cried out, my body quivering in pure desire.

Shane groaned, and after another thrust, he came. His torso folded over mine and I embraced him as he rode down his ecstasy, his body trembling even more than mine.

"I hope that was good," I teased. I was damn glad I hadn't exploded or hurt him.

He pulled back, staring at my eyes as if I was crazy. "It was fantastic, and you know it."

I chuckled. "Then hurry up and recover," I half-joked. We

had to take advantage of the control I still had. "I want round two."

He pulled back, eyes narrowed. "Are you sure about that?" The same question from before.

"I think so ... if you hurry."

Groaning, Shane buried his face on my neck. "Five minutes, then your wish is my desire."

25

RAIKA

I FELT GUILTY FOR NOT TELLING SHANE ABOUT THE PLAN yesterday, but if I had, we wouldn't have had such a great night. He would have freaked out, we would have argued, I would have slept in the castle by myself, and only today would he come groveling and say he was sorry. It was his nature as an alpha wolf—to get angry first, then to think through it all.

I rolled over in bed and looked at him.

"Good morning," he mumbled, his eyes still closed. He wound his arm around my waist and pulled me closer to him.

My body molded against his and I placed a kiss on his chin. "Morning."

"Isn't it too early? Let's go back to sleeping."

I chuckled. "It's almost eight in the morning." And I still needed to have breakfast, visit Ivy, and then go practice with Kaz. Our session last afternoon was cut short since I went to talk to Drake and the others.

Kaz wasn't a good teacher—he didn't speak a lot and seemed to be mad all the time—but he had shown me some cool tricks: how to mix both magics to enhance the dragon's magic powers and make more powerful strikes.

The first time I sent a bolt to a magical practice dummy, I jumped back, shocked with the explosion and how fast it disintegrated. The other time ... it had been fun.

I wondered what he would teach me today.

A phone vibrated. I reached for mine, Shane reached for his ... and both of us had the same text from Drake.

Meeting in thirty minutes.

Shane grunted. "They must have a plan."

"Yup." I rolled out of bed, feeling guilty. I cleaned up, brushed my teeth, dressed in black shorts and a top, and then faced Shane while he put on his pants and shirt.

He tilted his head. "Everything okay?"

I bit my lower lip. It would be best if he heard it from me, right? If Drake told us all during the meeting in a few minutes, he would be pissed.

"Shane, I know what the plan is," I blurted.

He zipped up his pants, stopped, frowned. "How?"

"It was my idea."

"What do you mean?"

"Tomorrow, I'll be Paimon's bait."

Shane's frown deepened, his jaw popped, the muscles on his arms tensed.

"Paimon wants my magic; he's obsessed with it. If we dangle me at the end of a stick, he won't resist it. He'll come. And then we attack and I kill him."

His eyes shone bright for a second. Shit, he was losing it.

"Fuck this," he muttered. He walked past me, to the door.

"Where are you going?" I asked, but he didn't answer. Shane left and the door closed with a loud bang. I flinched.

That had gone well.

Hopefully, he had gone for a run. That would help him calm down.

I took a deep breath and went to the conference room. Only Almae, Elisa, and Zadkiel were here so far. But others soon arrived—Killian and Lavinia, Kaz, Prince Cain, Prince Dorian, and Prince Aston. And then Thea and Drake.

From the head of the table, Drake looked around. "Where's Shane?"

"He ... he's not coming," I said, my voice tight.

Drake nodded. "All right. You can fill him in later." He glanced at us. "We have a plan and we're enacting it tomorrow morning."

"What is it?" Killian asked.

"We use Raika as bait," Drake said. Everyone looked at me as Drake went on about the plan. "Tomorrow morning, Raika will be near one of Paimon's abandoned buildings by herself. We'll start spreading the word tonight that Raika left the castle again and is searching for someone. He'll come to take her power away and—"

"Wait," Dorian said. "We tried this before with the gate. He only sent us two dead demon hunters."

I shook my head. "He's desperate for my power."

"I thought he was smart," Dorian said again.

"He is but he also knows I left the castle not three days ago to rescue my sister because he dangled her in front of me. He knows I would do it again if it was something important to me. And the last time, we lured him right to the gates. He knew something was up."

Drake nodded. "Exactly. And this is probably our last chance to lure him and play this game by our rules. After this, we'll need to prepare for open war and we might not have the manpower to do that."

My throat became dry. This was all on me. They were counting on me. I could do it. I would have to do it.

"We should spend the rest of the day training," Thea suggested. Kaz and I nodded.

"Good," Drake said. "Meanwhile, we'll gather our army, meet with the demon hunters, nail down the details, and get ready for tomorrow." He stood up. "Let's get to work."

After sharing a quick kiss with Thea, Drake left the room, with Prince Cain, Prince Dorian, Prince Aston, and Killian on his tail. Almae, Elisa, and Lavinia said they would gather the Silverblood witches, get them ready for tomorrow. Zadkiel said he would head to the underworld gate and help the demon hunters.

Then it was just me, Thea, and Kaz.

Kaz nudged his head toward the door. "Ready?"

Not really, but that wouldn't change anything.

THE DAY WAS HOTTER THAN USUAL, THE SUN BAKING US ALIVE IN the clearing. I had put on some sunscreen and pulled my long hair into a high ponytail. Kaz didn't seem bothered by the sun. Being a dragon shifter, he probably liked the heat. Thea didn't look bothered either, but under that fancy gown, she had to be. If it were me, I would be sweating buckets.

"Focus," Kaz said. He stood four feet from me, his feet apart and his hands raised, as if we would brawl instead of conjure magic. "Catch!"

He threw a quick bolt of dragon's magic—in his hands, it looked like fire. I took a step back, lifted my hands, and stopped it. The bolt, now a white flame, hovered over my hand.

I wiggled my fingers and the flame sparked with the movement. "This will not be enough."

On the way here, Thea and I told Kaz about the idea I had, of having some kind of spell Paimon wasn't expecting, that would take him by surprise, and would also be powerful enough to stop him.

"What about your fake army?" Kaz asked.

In ten seconds, Thea conjured ten bluish figures and I made ten more, all of them a mix of darkfire and dragon's magic.

"This might take Paimon by surprise, and keep his demons occupied so I can deal with him, but I'm not sure it's enough." I lowered my hand and the soldiers evaporated into thin air.

Kaz frowned. "What is unique to you? What can only you do?"

There was nothing unique to me, about me, and there was nothing only I could do, not when compared to everyone else. But maybe, when compared to Paimon ...

I gasped as an idea bloomed in my mind. "I know."

"What is it?" Thea asked.

"I ..." I smiled. "I'll show you. Though, you might want to stand back, in case this goes wrong."

Thea and Kaz took several steps back.

I turned my back to them and took my clothes off. They would still see my bare ass, but I was guessing that with Kaz being a shifter, he was used to nakedness. Wolf shifters should be, but I didn't really like anyone other than Shane seeing me naked.

I shifted into my dark gray wolf and turned back to them. I let out a short howl and then closed my eyes. I focused on the magic inside of me. Both of them were still strong when I was in this form. All I had to do was call to them and use them as I did when I was in human form.

Like before, both magics flooded my veins in an exhilarating rush. I inhaled and molded them to my desire. The skin under my fur warmed, growing slightly orange.

"Raika," Thea called out, probably seeing that I was heating up.

I took two steps back. This was still part of the plan.

I exhaled. Starting from my chest, my gray fur turned into flames, and in a few seconds, I was covered in flames.

"A fire wolf," Kaz whispered, his eyes wide.

The power within me, around me, was incredible. I could feel the flames, but not their heat. My sight was now sharper, my hearing even better, and I felt like I could run across the country in one go and not get tired at all.

I ran around the clearing, glad that even though I was on fire, the ground didn't catch it. I went back to center and tested that theory. I focused on one paw and imagined a bolt of magic there. When I pulled my paw back, the bolt was there. The fire started spreading, but I stepped over it and smothered it.

"Incredible," Thea said.

"Can you breathe fire?" Kaz asked.

My eyes widened. I hadn't thought of that. I turned away from them, aimed at a tree that was a little farther apart from the others, opened my mouth, and imagined myself spewing pure fire.

Nothing happened.

I looked at Kaz and shook my head.

Thea conjured one of her soldiers in front of me. "Attack him."

I jumped over the figure. Fire caught on him instantly,

burning him down in three seconds flat. The figure disappeared with a sizzling sound.

"We can't know that's what will happen with a supernatural, but that's pretty good," Kaz said. "This might work."

Was it me or did he sound pleased? As if he was about to smile?

I was so damn happy. I jumped around the clearing, celebrating that I finally had something Paimon wouldn't expect, and now I had a chance of actually killing him.

It happened fast. One second I was okay, the next my chest hurt and the heat became too much, even for me. The magic shook inside of me, unstable and uncontrollable.

I yelped and started retreating, but there was nowhere to go, and I wasn't fast enough. The flames sparked wide. I was going to explode.

The last thing I saw was a dragon shifter, with his wings wide open, lunging at me.

I groaned and rolled in bed.

But this wasn't my bed.

I sat up, confused for a second. My head spun and I was out of breath. Then it all came back to me—the training, the fire wolf, losing control, and Kaz running toward me.

"How are you feeling?" Shane asked. I turned to my right. There he was, seated on a chair beside my bed at the infirmary, his face worn and relieved.

I thought for a second. "Weak, dizzy, a little nauseous."

He nodded. "I was told you might feel like that when you woke up."

"What about Kaz? He threw himself at me!"

"I'm fine," Kaz said from the left. He was several feet away, beside the window. The sunlight streaking through the glass gave him a golden shine. He stepped closer. "I shifted and shielded you with my wings. The explosion was contained and no one got hurt."

"Thea is fine?"

Kaz nodded. "Yeah. She was here until a few minutes ago. She and I examined you, made sure you're all right, then she left to talk to some witches."

"Good," I whispered. Though I didn't feel well. I had finally found something I could fight Paimon with and I had lost control. This sucked big time. "How long have I been out?"

"A couple of hours," Kaz answered. "It's past lunchtime, actually, and Chef Morris asked me to tell him when you're awake, so ..." He gestured to the door. He marched out without another word or glance back.

I stilled in bed.

Shane stood and held my hand in his. "Kaz told me about the fire wolf. That probably looks incredible."

I frowned. He had walked out on me this morning. I didn't expect anything less from my mate, but shouldn't we talk about us before anything else?

I pulled my hand from his. "You walked out on me again."

He groaned. "I know, and I feel like a jerk."

"You were a jerk."

"I know. I have no fucking excuse. I got mad you went behind my back and planned everything with Drake without telling me about it."

"It was a sudden thing. I didn't plan on it. I just ... had the idea and went after Drake right then. And then ..." Shit, I was partly responsible here, wasn't I? "I didn't tell you last night because I wanted to enjoy the barbecue with you instead of arguing and agonizing about what might happen." This time, I reached for his hand and he let me have it. "I'm sorry. It's my fault too."

"It's okay." He leaned into me and pressed a kiss to my forehead. "We're fine, Raika. I might get mad sometimes, and you might be too impulsive, but we're fine, aren't we? Our love is stronger than that."

"Damn right," I whispered.

He brought his lips to mine in a soft, barely there kiss. I wanted to hold on to him, to ask for more, but I was too damn tired for that. This last explosion had taken a lot out of me.

I scooted to the side and Shane sat down beside me. He leaned on the headboard, his arm wide to the side, and I lay back, half on his chest, half on his arm.

"What now? I'm supposed to stay in bed for how long?" I asked.

"Thea said she would come back and check on you later, but from the quick exam she did, she thought you would be spent the rest of the day." He looked down at me. "Are you?"

I sighed. "I am." I nestled my head on his shoulder. "I might take a nap right here."

He chuckled. "I'm your personal pillow, blanket, mattress, whatever you need."

I turned more to him, my face on his neck, his musk and mint scent in my nostrils. I was so tired, I could sleep for a thousand years like this.

At some point, Chef Morris brought my lunch—and Shane's. Apparently, he hadn't eaten yet because he wanted to wait for me. I napped some more, and then later in the afternoon, Thea and Almae came in to check on me.

"I can feel your energy levels draining away," Almae said. "Like there's a leak on your gas tank."

That wasn't good. "Are you saying I'm dying faster?"

Almae and Thea exchanged a dark look. "We can't say for sure, maybe Kaz can," Thea said. "But we know the last burst burned through a lot of your energy and the dragon's magic is taking over."

I sucked in a sharp breath. "Will I be able to do what I have to tomorrow?"

"We hope so," Almae said. "Kaz is helping us make an elixir to give you a burst of energy for when the time comes."

Shane stiffened beside me. "Won't that burn through her energy faster later?"

"It might," Thea said. She looked at me. "It's a risk and a choice only you can make."

Almae patted my leg. "You should focus on resting. We'll come check on you later."

The two of them headed to the door, when it opened suddenly and Killian rushed in.

"Here you are," he said, his grave eyes on Thea. "Drake is looking for you."

Thea rushed out at once, and Almae followed her.

Killian turned to us, his eyes grave. "Shane, we might need your help."

Shane stood from the bed. "What is it?"

"Paimon started a full attack on one of the gates."

The blood rushed from my face. "What?"

"We need every hand we can get," Killian said.

Shane looked at me.

"Wait for me." I scooted to the edge of the bed and as I sat up, a wave of dizziness assaulted me.

Shane held my arm. "You can't go, Raika. You're too weak."

"But I have to! If this is it, then I have to be there!"

"Raika," Killian started, his voice low. "I actually have orders from Lord Drake. You're to stay here and rest. In a couple of hours, someone will come back to check on you. If by then you're feeling better, then you can join us."

I stared at Shane and Killian. "Drake isn't my alpha. I don't have to listen to him." I pushed from the bed. Instantly, my knees wobbled and my vision darkened.

Shane picked me up before I kissed the ground. He deposited me in bed. "Raika, Drake is right. You need to stay and rest." I looked at him, at his pleading eyes. "Please, stay. Rest."

I punched his shoulder. "You can't do this to me. I need to be there."

"You'll only get yourself killed faster." He pointed to the floor. "Didn't you see what happened? You can barely stand on your own." He grabbed my nape and rested his forehead on mine. "Please, stay. Don't make me use my alpha command on you."

I gasped. "You wouldn't."

"To keep you safe? Yes, I would." I grabbed his wrist. "I'll come back in a couple of hours, okay? Just ... stay here." He pressed a kiss to my forehead, then rushed out of the room. Killian was gone half a second later with his damn vampire speed.

And I was left alone in the infirmary like an invalid.

26

SHANE

It killed me to leave Raika behind, but with Paimon attacking a portal with all his forces, it meant we needed to hit him with everything and everyone we had. Especially because it seemed Raika wouldn't be able to do her part.

We would find a way to kill him. I would find a way.

As I raced through the castle's hallways, weaving through the many vampires and witches rushing outside, where warlocks had opened up portals to take us to the battle ground, I texted Dom, Lucille, Hamill, and the others. I told them to come quick and help.

I also texted Tyren, ordering him to stay in the village and take care of the pack while we were gone. Of course, he called me right back and yelled at me, but I reminded him, "One beta has to stay with the pack. Plus, I only trust you to take care of Minsi and Raika if anything goes wrong."

That shut him up.

I walked by one of the weapons rooms strategically hidden around the castle and paused. I didn't need any weapons, but maybe I could take a few grenades or spell bombs and throw them before shifting. I found an empty satchel, filled it up with plenty of bombs, then joined the throng of supernaturals outside.

Drake and Thea stood to the side, coordinating the mess. Killian and the other princes stood beside the portals, telling supernaturals to cross and turn either right or left on the other side. Lavinia stood beside Killian, waiting for her turn to go through.

I approached the portals as the crowd crossed over. Then Dom, Lucille, Hamill, and a handful of others arrived to join me.

"Everything okay at the village?" I asked.

Dom nodded. "Rue and Lydia were warned of what's happening."

I frowned.

Lucille touched my arm. "The fight is elsewhere. They will be fine."

I looked down at her. It wasn't long ago that she was shallow and only cared about her looks. Now she was here, ready to go into battle with our pack. I was proud of her.

I opened my mouth to say as much, but then it was our turn.

Killian grasped my shoulder and I paused in front of the portal. "Go to the left. That's where I'll be going once I'm through."

I nodded and walked through the portal.

The ground shook and a loud boom echoed through the air. I stared at the scene in front of me—pure chaos.

It was like one of those medieval battle scenes from movies—two thick walls pushing against each other, one made of supernaturals, the other made of demons and some hideous creatures—the Huddyriuns Raika had told us about.

"Go!" someone yelled behind me.

I lowered my head and turned left, as instructed. I weaved through the crowd, moving right behind one of those walls, and with the gate to the underworld behind us.

I saw a few faces I knew spread out: Hadrian, Rey, Erin, Ariella, Kaz, Norah, Doreen, and many others. Most of the high-ranking supernaturals weren't in the thick of the fight, and I knew why.

"I don't see him," I said, looking around.

Dom scanned the crowd. "Paimon? I don't see him either."

A darkfire zipped toward us and we ducked. The bolt exploded on the ground not ten feet behind us.

Ariella joined us, panting. I had seen her almost at the front line, taking down demons with ease. "He's not here."

I balked at her. "What?"

"He came in with the first wave," she said. "He taunted us, and when the battle started, he retreated. Hadrian thinks he's behind their portal, biding his time while his demons kill us."

"But we're killing them too, right?" Lucille asked.

Ariella nodded. "It's been a balanced battle so far. No one has gained any ground."

I frowned. Paimon had taunted everyone here and then he didn't use his magic to stop us and take the underworld for himself? Was that how these big fights usually went? With the bad guy hiding and letting everyone else kill themselves first?

A chill ran down my spine. "Where's King Tanner?"

"I don't know," Ariella said. "They have been quiet about that for days now. Word is that Tanner wanted to fight, but Jasmin and Erin took him to a safe location until this is over."

"What if this takes days, weeks?" Kaz asked.

Ariella shrugged. "I don't make decisions. I just come to help and do what I'm told."

So Tanner was safe. Even if Paimon's plan was to distract everyone here and go after Tanner, he wouldn't be able to, unless—

A huge wave of darkfire rushed through the crowd. Most of us had time to duck, but the front line was hit full on and dozens of demon hunters dropped to the ground.

The demons stopped fighting.

Rotgar appeared behind them, as if standing on a stage. Maybe he was.

With a wicked smile, he scanned the crowd. "My dead heart is so content to see all of you here this evening." His voice boomed through the air, amplified by magic.

"Cut the crap!" Ariella shouted, just as loud.

His eyes met hers. "Oh, the fallen angel. Have you recovered your wings yet, sweetheart?"

Ariella's face grew red.

Drake advanced a few steps through the fallen crowd, with Thea, Hadrian, Rey, Erin, and several others flanking him. "Where's Paimon?"

Rotgar turned his fake smile to the vampire lord. "Oh, I see you care. Don't worry, he is fine."

"Where is he?" Drake repeated. "Is he such a coward he won't face us?"

"Paimon is busy right now, but I brought two of his brothers to play with you." He gestured to the portal behind him and two forms stepped through.

A hush fell over the demon hunters.

I frowned. "Who are those?"

"Prince Maggoth and Prince Zeltov," Ariella said. "Former princes of the underworld, just like Paimon."

Shit. It seemed he had gotten some powerful allies.

The princes launched themselves into the crowd and the fight restarted.

Something tugged in the back of my mind. Rotgar said Paimon was busy. With what? Wasn't this more important than anything else to him?

No.

I went still.

There was something he had wanted for some time now, something new and shiny and that he had tried getting before.

Raika's dragon magic.

Paimon wasn't here. He wasn't even coming.

While we were all here distracted, he acted.

Paimon was going after Raika.

27

RAIKA

I felt like a rebellious teen who had done something bad, got grounded, and had to stay in her bedroom the rest of the day. Alone in the infirmary, I pouted and stomped side to side—when I could stand. The dizziness and weakness came and went, but sometimes it took me under. I had napped twice this afternoon already, and even though it was still early in the evening, I was considering napping again or going to sleep and hopefully waking up at a decent time tomorrow.

I stayed in bed, with my phone in my hands, waiting for news.

But time crawled and nothing happened.

Suddenly, my phone rang. I jumped but frowned when I saw the name on the screen.

"Hi, Rue, everything okay?" I asked.

"No," she said, her voice trembling. "Minsi is having a panic attack. The bunny isn't working, and I don't know what else to do. She's losing it."

My heart clenched. "All right. I'll be there soon." Panic

attacks didn't last long, so hopefully, by the time I got there, Minsi would already be all right.

I reached to the bedside table where the elixir and the tablet were—I took one of each, hoping they would stave off the dragon's magic and give me a little boost so I didn't faint before I reached the door. I decided to take two more with me, just in case I stayed there. and slipped the vial and the pill into my shorts' pocket.

Slowly, I got out of bed and I didn't feel dizzy, though my legs wobbled. I held on to the headboard and took a deep breath, steading myself. I could do this! I walked to the door, and with each step, I felt a little stronger, a little steadier.

The castle's hallways were empty. Almost everyone had left to help defend the underworld gate. I passed one guard stationed at the castle's underground garage and he asked me where I was going.

"Minsi is having a panic attack," I told him. Everyone knew about Minsi by now. He nodded, understanding. I frowned. "Any news?"

He shook his head. "I don't think we'll hear anything for a while."

I nodded, thanked him, grabbed the keys to a car, and moved on. I hopped inside a Jeep and drove to the village. I didn't think I was in any condition to drive or walk there, but driving would be a lot faster and easier.

Like the castle, the village was eerily quiet and empty. Shane must have taken all of the strongest wolves to the battle with him.

It hurt to stay behind.

I parked the car in front of our house and walked to the door. Hoping the door was unlocked because I had no idea where my keys were, I turned the knob and pushed it open.

Everything was dark and quiet. "Rue?" I called as I stepped in. "Minsi?" I turned into the bedrooms' hallway. "Tyren?" The doors were open but no one was here.

I picked up my phone from my back pocket and called Rue back. I heard a faint ring, but ... it wasn't coming from inside. Following the low ringing, I dragged my tired feet to the kitchen. It was louder here, but not loud enough. I opened the backdoor and stepped out into the porch.

My heart stopped.

"No," I whispered.

"Hello, dear daughter." Paimon smiled at me from the middle of the backyard—with Minsi, Tyren, and Rue kneeling in front of him, facing me, their hands tied behind their backs and a darkfire gag over their mouths. He placed a hand on Tyren's shoulder and the boy flinched.

Rage coursed through me. "Let them go! Your fight is with me!"

"I fight dirty," Paimon said, proud of himself.

I clenched my hands. "So this was your plan? To distract the others at the gate while you came here? Why? I thought what you wanted the most was to get the underworld back."

"Oh, it is, but after what happened with the dragon's magic, I realized I need all of it." He flexed his hands and a swirl of dragon magic enveloped his arms. "When I have it all, I'll be the most powerful supernatural in the world, and taking the underworld back will be easy." He shrugged. "So I added a pitstop to my original plan."

My gut twisted. I was weak, I had taken the two medicines that numbed the dragon's magic, and I was alone. Face-to-face against Paimon like this meant certain death.

But I was dying anyway. If I could take him with me, great. If I couldn't, then maybe I could at least wound him, or weaken him to the point where the others could finish him when they arrived here. Because they would, right? At some point they would realize the battle they were fighting was a distraction and Paimon was really here.

I just hoped they weren't too late.

I had to buy us some time.

"Let them go," I repeated. "Then you can have me."

Minsi cried and Tyren's eyes widened. He jerked and tried coming up, but Paimon easily pushed him down and kept him down, probably with magic.

Rage like I never knew before filled my veins. This man, my terrible father, was hurting my family. I would make sure he regretted it.

"If I let them go, who says you won't change your mind?" Paimon asked. "There's no fun in that. Speaking of fun, should we dial it up?" He grabbed something from his pocket —the key.

A green portal opened several feet behind him and demons spilled out. Dozens of them. I gawked as the demons spread out around us, forming a wide circle.

A circle.

I frowned, remembering Thea and Almae had drawn a witch's circle to contain my power in case I lost it. Could it be used to hurt someone inside? I filed that idea aside for when backup arrived.

"You." Paimon gestured to a group of demons to his right. "Go to the main road. Stop anyone who gets close." The demons nodded, grunted, and marched away.

My heart tugged. There were pack members in their houses, most of them getting ready for bed, clueless of what was happening. If they saw something odd, they might come out, and the demons would attack them.

I gritted my teeth. This was going too far. "Paimon, stop this," I said.

He tilted his head. "What happened to father?"

"You might be my biological father, but you don't deserve being called one," I spat.

He pressed a hand to his chest, pretending to be hurt. The prick. He loved theatrics. "You wound me, my daughter."

I rolled my eyes. "Cut the crap, Paimon. Let them go. Then you can have me."

"Don't you get it?" He waved his hand and a snake of dragon magic floated toward me. "I can have you right now with or without them." The snake wrapped around me. "I was already stronger than you before, and I'm still stronger than you are now. Whatever plan you're coming up with in your mind, don't bother. You can't win."

But I could stall until the others arrived. At least the portal had closed and no more demons came through.

I put a hand on my waist. "What is the dragon magic doing for you?"

That got his attention. His brows dipped slightly. "What do you mean?"

"The dragon magic is killing me. Isn't it affecting you?"

His brows curled some more. "You're dying?"

I nodded. "But what do you care. Once you take the dragon's magic from me, you'll kill me anyway, won't you?"

His eyes darkened.

Screams came from the street. Grunts and howls sounded next. Shit, the pack members. "Stop it!" I called out to Paimon. "Tell them to stop hurting my pack. Here." I took two steps closer to him and offered him my hands. "Take me, just ... don't hurt anyone."

He stared at me for a moment. "This is war. A lot of people will get hurt."

A growl came from my throat and I called my magic—the dragon magic was mostly numb, but I had awoken it before and I would do it again.

In the span of two seconds, I threw darkfire at Minsi, Tyren, and Rue, an exact hit to break the holds of Paimon's darkfire on them. Then I threw an onslaught of dragon magic's bolts at Paimon, mostly to distract him while Rue grabbed Minsi and they ran for the house, and Tyren jumped up and stood beside me.

Demons blocked Rue and Minsi's path, and they ended up right behind Tyren and me.

I threw bolts at Paimon and Tyren shifted, ripping through his clothes. Behind us, Rue shifted too and Minsi crouched down, her hands over her ears and her eyes closed tight.

Paimon laughed as he swept his hand in the air and deflected my bolts. "This is pathetic, Raika. I thought you could do better."

I could. I just didn't want to waste energy, not yet.

"I'll say it one more time: let them go." There was a bite to my words.

Paimon's amused mask fell and he glowered at me. "You insolent child." He threw his dragon magic at me. I pushed Tyren out of the way and ran to the other side, just a couple of steps, enough to get away from the strike and from the others.

But he didn't turn to me. He turned to Tyren. The teenage wolf snarled and jumped at Paimon. Paimon stepped back and let a wave of darkfire hit Tyren's side. He flew several feet back and fell hard on the ground with a yelp.

"No!" I screamed, my rage gaining new heights.

I focused on my magic. It was time to call the fire wolf. It was my only chance. With renewed energy, I ran toward the forest beyond the backyard. If he followed me, I could shift into the fire wolf, and if I lost control, I wouldn't hurt anyone else.

I took only three steps and froze in place when a whirlwind of dragon magic swirled around me. The whirlwind pushed me back until I was facing Paimon, two feet from him.

"I told you there was no reason for you to fight me," he said, leaning over me. "I will always win." He closed his hand around my throat and pulled me up, my feet dangling in the air. I gasped for air. "Now, say goodbye."

He started absorbing my magic.

28

SHANE

LIKE A MANIAC, I CUT THROUGH THE CROWD, UNTIL I FOUND Drake and Thea—they had crossed through the portal and joined the chaos on this side.

I skidded to a stop beside them. "He went after Raika," I blurted out.

Drake stared me. "Paimon? But ..." His eyes widened. "This is a distraction."

I nodded.

"Oh, no." Thea put both hands over her mouth. "And the castle is under protected."

"Shit." Drake looked around. He made a beeline to the back of our army. I followed him and it was only then that I noticed there were more people following me—Dom, Lucille, Hamill, Kaz, Ariella, Norah, and Doreen.

"What's going on?" Ariella asked, but I waved her off. I was too wound up to talk right now.

Drake halted in front of Aspen, who had been ordered to stay at the back, where he could open the portal again in case we needed to evacuate.

"Open a portal to DuMoir," Drake ordered.

Without hesitation, Aspen did as asked. Drake turned to me. "Go. Take your friends. I'll send Prince Cain and his vampires to help you." He grasped my shoulder. "I'll be there soon. First, we need to deal with the princes and demons here."

I nodded, understanding. They couldn't abandon everything here and go after Paimon, or they would take this advantage to invade the underworld and still win.

I walked through the portal and came out in front of DuMoir Castle, my friends beside me.

"Where is he?" Norah asked.

I frowned. The castle was too quiet and there was no sign of Paimon. I ran alongside the castle, trying to spot a battle or some disturbance, but there was nothing.

I saw a guard patrolling the underground garage and ran to him. "Where's Paimon?"

The vampire frowned at me. "Paimon here? No, everything is quiet in the castle."

That couldn't be. I knew I wasn't wrong. Unless ...

"What about Raika? Have you seen her?"

He nodded. "Yes, she left about thirty minutes ago. Took a car and went to the village. Something about your sister having a panic attack."

"That's Paimon," Ariella said. "He used Minsi as bait."

Oh, hell no. A growl ripped through my throat as I ran and shifted mid-stride. My clothes ripped into pieces and fell to the ground. I pumped my legs as fast as I could, leaving my friends behind.

Don't go in there alone, Dom said in my mind.

Wait for us, Hamill said.

If it's a trap, then don't fall for it, Lucille added. *Be smart!*

Smart? Right now? All I could think about was getting my hands around Paimon's throat and ripping it open. It was a shame that might not kill him. But I would find a way, because tonight, I would put an end to him.

The flap of wings sounded overheard—Kaz in his dragon shifter form, flying toward the village. Apparently, I wouldn't be the first one to get there.

A scream echoed from the village and I ran faster. My legs faltered when I saw a handful of wolves fighting a dozen demons in the street in front of my house. They were here. They were really here.

A bright light came from the back of the house.

There.

I wanted to stay and help everyone, but I couldn't. I had to make choices and right now, Raika was it. I turned to the side of the house and went to the back.

The scene in front of me almost paralyzed me—a circle of demons in the backyard. Rue in her wolf form, her side bleeding as she snapped at demons trying to advance on a crying Minsi. Tyren in his wolf form on the ground several feet to the side, unmoving. And Paimon right in the center, holding Raika by her throat.

And absorbing her magic?

I pushed harder, broke through the wall of demons around the backyard, and jumped at Paimon's side.

He lost his grip on Raika and she fell to the ground. Before he could turn to her again, I lunged at him and bit his arm. Paimon screamed. He pushed his hand out and a dark-fire bolt zipped to me. I twisted my body, but not enough. The bolt grazed my shoulder and I yelped, letting go of him.

I growled at him, ready to go again.

A light bolt zipped through the air and hit Paimon in the

chest. He scrambled back and my friends ran at him. The demons surged forward, trying to stop their attack, and I realized this gave me a breather.

I turned to Raika.

She sat up with a groan as I leaned over her. She reached up and caressed my neck as I nuzzled her. "I'm fine," she said, her voice weak. "Not in the best shape, but fine." She rested her head on mine. "I knew you were coming."

I licked her cheek and she smiled at me.

A grunt came from the side and I took a moment to look around. Kaz and Ariella fought Paimon, while Hamill and Lucille helped Rue with the demons, and Dom checked on Tyren. My brother stood on shaky legs.

Tyren, are you okay? I asked through the mind link.

I'll survive, he said.

Norah and Doreen had stayed back, trying to contain the demons in front of the house, but now they all ran back—and Prince Cain and five of his vampires zoomed alongside them.

The battle around us intensified.

Paimon threw a wave of dragon magic at us. We all jumped back, trying to avoid it. He then used that second to open a green portal behind him—and those ugly creatures stepped out from it.

Shit. *Rue and Lucille, get Minsi out of here,* I ordered. *Dom and Hamill, let's get these monsters. Tyren, stay with Raika.*

Yelps of agreement sounded in the night.

Dom, Hamill, and I joined the others trying to contain the demons and Huddyriuns who kept surging from the portal with their crude weapons—how many freaking allies did Paimon have?

I wanted to switch my attention back to Paimon, but with so many enemies attacking us, it would be impossible.

A Huddyriuns kicked Norah in the chest and the powerful beast sent her flying back. She fell like a heap of dirt at Paimon's feet. Paimon didn't hesitate. He grabbed Norah by the throat and threw her like a fly—directly into the portal.

"Norah!" Cain shouted. He zipped after her.

The portal closed.

I growled, finishing off the demon I had been fighting, and tried turning back to Paimon. Three more demons jumped over me, staving off my efforts.

What the fuck?

Paimon yelled, "Enough!"

He brought his hands up, creating a round shield of dragon magic around him, Kaz, Ariella, Raika, and Tyren.

I rushed toward it, but the shield held, and I bounced back. It was like hitting a concrete wall.

"That is enough," Paimon said with a snarl.

Kaz lunged at him, but he threw several darts of darkfire at him. Kaz tried maneuvering out of the way, but a few darts went through his wings and one hit his chest. He went down with a cry.

Ariella sent her light magic at Paimon, but he created a darkfire shield, and let them explode. Then he sent the shield toward the fallen angel. Ariella jumped out of the way and right into Paimon's hands. He wrapped her in darkfire and grabbed her head with both hands.

"Now, your magic will be mine," he said.

"No!" Raika yelled. She cast a huge dragon magic bolt and threw it at Paimon's side. He clambered, but didn't lose his grip on Ariella. The angel fought against his hold, but her light magic floated from her face to his, and she was visibly weakening.

Raika attacked again and then Tyren jumped on Paimon's back. He bit down on Paimon's shoulder. The demon hollered and shook his body, until Tyren fell back. He kicked Tyren in the ribs. My brother whined as he tried to get up.

Raika rushed Paimon. She shoved her hands at his face. He blinked, confused—I was too, what the hell was she doing? The demon finally let go of Ariella, and the angel fell to the ground like a sack of potatoes.

Paimon screamed as Raika retreated a few steps. He wiped at his face. "What the hell is this?"

"The elixir and the medicine that inhibit the dragon magic," she said. Her hands dripped blood. She had broken the vial in his face! "The thing is, I trained to be able to call my magic even after having taken the elixirs. You haven't."

She threw a big bolt of both darkfire and dragon magic at Paimon.

He fell back and I jumped up in the air. *Yes!*

The barrier around them sparked, but held. It wouldn't last long, though.

A demon tackled me and I lost sight of their fight. When I killed the demon and looked again, I saw figures made of both darkfire and dragon magic surrounding Paimon. He strained to get a hold of his magic, but couldn't. The dragon's magic flickered in his hands, then went off. He fought against the figures, mostly with punches and kicks.

Raika glanced at me and the others. "Everyone, step back!"

I frowned.

Then she shifted. *Remember the witch's circle?* she asked in my mind. *The shield will fall and you need to make sure our friends are out of range.*

Out of range? For what?

For this.

Flames covered her fur and I gasped. This woman didn't cease to amaze me.

She lunged at Paimon, taking him down. The barrier fell. I hesitated for two seconds, then remembered what she said.

Push everyone back, away from the witch's circle, I told my wolves.

I ran to Tyren, helped him up, and walked with him until he was outside the hidden witch's circle. Then I went back for Ariella. For a second, I thought Paimon had killed her, but I could hear her slow heartbeat and ragged breathing. I bit down on the corner of her sleeve and pulled her outside the circle. Kaz dragged himself back and tackled a demon, even though he was hurt and weak.

I went around, helping the others and making sure all of our friends were a good distance from the backyard.

Then I stopped and turned to the center. It took everything in me to stand there and do nothing as Paimon grappled with Raika, trying to call his magic and failing.

My body wanted to move, to go in the circle and help her, but I knew that if she lost control of the dragon's magic, I would be toast, and she wouldn't. Hopefully.

More vampires arrived and dealt with the demons, while I watched as Raika jumped on Paimon and pinned him down, the flames of her body flickering high and wide.

Paimon screamed as a white light emanated from his skin and floated toward Raika. She was absorbing his magic! If she did that, if she took his entire magic, he would be a powerless demon and easier to kill.

He jerked under her paws, but somehow Raika's fire wolf was too strong and getting stronger. Paimon was no match for her like this. She inhaled, taking the last of his magic.

Paimon went still.

Raika stepped away from him, the flames around her body higher than ever, sparking loudly. She trembled and her breathing grew shallow.

I took a step forward—

"No." Kaz put an arm in front of me. He stood by my side, hurt and bloody, and back in his human form. "Don't go inside yet."

The fire grew bigger, the heat pushed against us.

She was going to explode again.

I yelped, hoping everyone understood what I meant. In my mind, I said to my pack, *retreat as much as you can!*

Her flames turned white and—

With a grunt, Paimon rolled to his knees, grabbed a dagger one of the Huddyriuns had dropped, and plunged it into Raika's stomach.

No!

I ran to her as the flames extinguish and Raika fell.

Paimon laughed, the bloody dagger in his hand. With a growl, I lunged at him, knocking the dagger from his hand, and closed my mouth around his neck. I squeezed as hard as I could while Paimon fought against my grip, his energy depleting fast. Even though I knew this wouldn't be enough to kill him, it brought me pure pleasure.

"Here," Raika whispered. Back in her human form, she extended her hand to me. I moved my body so she could touch my leg. Her power rushed through me and burst through my teeth. It flooded into Paimon.

He screamed.

Her dragon's magic burned him from the inside out. I opened my mouth and let him fall, his body limp, his eyes glassy.

I turned to Raika, my heart twisting. Blood oozed from her stomach and she convulsed.

No, please, dear moon, no. I scooted to her side, resting my head on her shoulder.

Under my fur, her skin heated up. I pulled back and stared at her orange skin. One second later, the flames erupted.

Wings surrounded me as the world became a sea of fire.

Then Kaz lowered his wings. The grass was gone in the witch's circle and a dark patch on the ground was all that was left from Paimon. And Raika lay on the grass, her heartbeat growing faint.

I shifted back to my human form. "Help!" I shouted. "We need a healer, a witch, someone!" I held her hand, suddenly so cold, and lowered my head to hers. "Please, Raika, don't go. Not yet."

29

RAIKA

I TRIED HOLDING ON TO CONSCIOUSNESS BUT I KEPT BLACKING out. I remembered Shane shifting back to human form, yelling for help. Him picking me up and running through the remainder of the battle to the car parked on the street. Then we were inside the castle, and he raced down the hallways.

Next, I was in the infirmary with Thea, Almae, Meredith, and Jay watching over me. They kept talking to me, but I couldn't make sense of any of it. At some point, Thea gave me something to help with the pain and relax me—at least, that was what I thought I heard. Next thing I knew, I fell into a deep sleep.

When I woke up, the sun was up and I was smooshed between Shane and Minsi—they had pushed another bed next to mine so they could be close to me. A smile tugged at my lips, but it was short-lived as a discomfort hit me hard within. Everything in me hurt, a dull and constant pain that seemed buried within my bones and muscles. My head throbbed harder and when I propped myself up on my elbows, my head spun and my sight blurred.

What the hell?

I frowned and thought of last night.

Paimon had tricked me. He had used Minsi, Tyren, and Rue to bait me, and it had worked. But my friends had come to help; Shane had come to help. I gasped, remembering I had taken Paimon's power—all of it. I hadn't done it on purpose.

In the end, even wounded, the dragon's magic burst from me and Paimon was obliterated. We had won.

Wounded! I placed a hand to my stomach, where Paimon had stabbed me. I wasn't feeling any pain. I lifted my shirt and found only a faint scar. Thank goodness for wolf healing and expert healers and potions!

I gasped again and looked at Shane. He had been there with me when I exploded. And yet ... he was here beside. I could hear his deep breathing, the steady, strong beat of his heart. He was fine.

I sat up a little more and glanced around.

Kaz was directly across the corridor formed by the beds, lying on his back, his torso bandaged. He had jumped in and covered Shane, like he had done with me in training.

Tyren slept on the bed beside mine and I sighed in relief. Paimon had hurt him, but he had fought bravely and he was fine now. I could see the up and down of his chest from here.

Then I saw Rue and Ariella in other beds. My heart squeezed. Rue had defended Minsi with all she had, and Ariella ... Paimon had taken her powers away. I glanced down at my hands. Did I have her powers now? Maybe I could return them.

I had not wanted the dragon's magic in the first place. I certainly didn't want Paimon's power, much less the power he had stolen from others.

There were more supernaturals in the infirmary—a handful of witches and even a couple of vampires. There wasn't one single empty bed in the entire room. I wondered ... with so many injured, were there any deaths? Of course, there were. War always brought death.

A sudden thought came to mind. What was I doing here with these other people? I should be isolated in case I lost control again. I couldn't be here and—

"Hey, you," Shane whispered.

I looked at him, my eyes wide. "Why am I not in my own room, far away from everyone else?"

"There's a witch's circle around these beds, and you were given the elixirs ..." He pulled his cell phone from the side and glanced at the screen. "Not two hours ago."

I relaxed a little, but not too much. When Thea or Meredith came to check on us, I would ask to leave. Now that I had all the dragon's magic, we didn't know if the witch's circle would be enough.

Though it had held during battle, hadn't it? At least, no one here seemed to have been burned by my fire.

A little less worried, I lay back down and turned to Shane.

He reached over and smoothed a hand over my arm. "How are you feeling?"

"Like I was run over by a military tank," I joked, though there was nothing funny about it. "How about you? Are you okay? Did I burn you?"

Shane shook his head. "Kaz did his thing."

I smiled. "Good. Remind me to thank him later."

His brows knotted. "Seriously now, how are you?"

I hesitated. There was no reason to lie. "Everything hurts and I feel like I might faint at any second."

He ran his fingers through my hair. "What you did last night ... it took a lot from you."

It did. I could feel it. I knew the timetable had moved. If before I had maybe two weeks to live, now I might have five days, at most. With each breath, I could feel the energy sapping from me.

"I had to," I said. "It was the only way."

"I know, and I'm proud of you."

That was good to know. But there were other things I wanted to know. "What happened at the other battle, the underworld gate?"

"Paimon sent Rotgar and two former princes, plus his demons and those Huddyriuns to attack us," Shane said, his tone somber. "Even though it was a distraction, demon hunters, vampires, witches, and warlocks were fighting to protect the gate."

Which meant, a lot of them were hurt. "How did it end?"

"When I realized Paimon's real objective, I left, so I didn't see what happened next, but Killian and Drake came in to check on the wounded in the middle of the night and told me." He paused. "They lost a lot of lives, but they held the line. The demons and the princes didn't get near the gate, and when they heard Paimon had fallen, they retreated as fast as they had come."

"So it's over?"

Shane nodded. "It seems to be, though the demon hunters won't ease security around the gates for a long while."

As they shouldn't. Who knew how many allies Paimon had out there? Some crazy demon might want to continue his plan and attack again. I shuddered, hoping that never happened.

A glimpse of the battle came back to mind and I inhaled deeply. "What happened to Norah and Prince Cain? Are they back?"

Shane shook his head. "Paimon threw Norah through the portal, Cain ran after her, and now no one can find the key to open the portal again. Either the key was stolen or destroyed during the explosion."

My chest deflated. Oh no, those two. They were now lost in a strange realm, going through who knew what ... at least they were together. And I was sure Drake wouldn't rest until he found a way to open the portal again and bring them back. Still, that didn't sit well with me.

Someone snuggled at my back and I gently turned. "Hey you." I opened my arms and Minsi nestled herself against me. "Are you okay?" She nodded, her chin grazing my collarbone. I kissed her forehead. "That is over. You'll never had to go through that again. I promise."

Shane spooned me from behind. I glanced over Minsi's head and found Tyren watching us. I beckoned him over. He hesitated, but came. He lay behind Minsi and reached over, his hand on my arm, and Shane put a big, heavy arm around all of us. Despite everything, contentment filled my heart, and with a soft smile, I fell asleep again.

***

"She's heating up again."

"Stay away from her."

"She needs to be moved somewhere else."

I blinked, but couldn't get a hold of myself, of my thoughts. I was drowning in fire, too hot to breath, to think.

"She'll be fine."

A hand pushed on my nape and then a cold liquid pooled at my mouth and dripped down my throat. I inhaled as the fire in my lungs, in my veins retreated. I wasn't bathing in fire anymore, but I was still too damn hot.

At least clarity seemed to return to me as I blinked and saw a crowd of people standing a few feet away, all of them behind the witch's circle, except for Meredith, Kaz, and Shane. Even the second bed had been pushed away from me, and Minsi and Tyren crouched over it, their worried eyes on me.

"Hey," I croaked, my throat dry. Shane helped me sit up, and Meredith propped some pillows behind my back. I was so, so weak, and still too hot. "They are right. I shouldn't be here."

"That's what the witch's circle is for," Meredith said.

"I still think I should go somewhere else," I insisted. "Maybe my previous room? It also has a witch's circle, and it's close to the infirmary, but not too close?" I wanted to go to a hut in the middle of the forest, where I couldn't hurt anyone, but I doubt they would let me.

Meredith's eyes narrowed. "I'll talk to Thea."

"Thank you," I whispered, too weak to talk properly.

Shane put a hand to my forehead and glanced at Kaz and Meredith. "Can she take another elixir? She's still burning up."

"The last one is still working through her system," Kaz said. "Give it a little time."

The supernaturals fanned out, most of them returning to their beds, except for Rue, who stood with Tyren and Minsi, looking at me with love-filled eyes. There was a purple bruise on her shoulder and neck, and she had a few scratches on her face, but other than that, she looked okay.

"Thank you," I said to her. "For standing up for Minsi."

She waved me off. "You know you're all my own children." The ones she never had because her mate died. My heart squeezed. "I would do anything for you." She frowned. "Even trade places with you, if I could."

Meredith shook her head. "You already asked, and I said it's impossible."

I gawked. Rue had asked that? The nerve! As if I would agree to something so ridiculous.

I looked beyond them and the empty bed there caught my attention. "Where's Ariella?"

Shane sighed. "She left."

"What? How? Wasn't she hurt?"

"She wouldn't let me examine her," Meredith said, sounding upset about it. "She woke up and left."

Kaz frowned. "First she lost her wings, now she lost her powers."

Shit, that was horrible. "I can't imagine what she's feeling right now."

"I understand the will to leave and hide," Kaz said, as if speaking from experience. We didn't know much about him and I didn't think we would.

Maybe she needed some time to accept the reality of it, but after a few days, someone needed to check on her. This could be affecting her a lot more than it seemed.

Meredith patted my arm. "All right, dear, you should rest."

"True," Shane agreed.

I wouldn't argue with that. I lay back and closed my eyes. "Please talk to Thea. I want to get out of here."

"Will do," Meredith said.

I held Shane's hand and without opening my eyes, I said,

"You should take Minsi and Tyren from here. They don't need to see me like this."

He leaned closer and whispered, "They want to be with you until ..." He clamped his mouth, not saying the words none of us wanted to hear—until I died.

Since I didn't have much time left, here they were. My heart clenched and tears burned behind my closed eyelids. I heard footsteps retreating, probably Meredith going to talk to Thea about moving me to a safer place.

Then the door opened and someone rushed in.

I opened my eyes as Killian glided to my bed, but his gaze was locked on Kaz. He saw me awake and spared me a glance. "Hey, you seem to be feeling better."

Hardly. "I am," I lied.

"Sorry, but this is kind of urgent." He turned back to Kaz. "Lyra is back from the goblins' mountain."

Kaz frowned. "And?"

"She and Etyx brought back dragon eggs."

30

RAIKA

Kaz's eyes widened so big, I thought they would swallow his entire face. "Dragon eggs?"

Killian nodded. "At least, that's what they think they are."

Kaz ran out of the room and Killian followed him.

I inhaled sharply. "The dragon was female. She had been imprisoned for so long while about to lay eggs." That was so freaking cruel. "When she got free, she found her babies' a nest." The mountain.

"What a turn of events," Shane mused. He looked up at Minsi and Tyren. "Why don't you two go take a look at the eggs? That will probably be a once-in-a-lifetime experience."

Minsi pouted. "I want to stay with Raika."

My jaw fell open and Shane froze.

That was the most she had spoken in over a year! A laugh bubbled from my chest, but I kept it down. I didn't want to scare her. "I know, pretty girl, but you can just go, take a peek, and come back. I promise I'll still be here when you come back."

She looked unsure, but Tyren coaxed her, and she finally moved. Rue went out with them.

I sighed in relief and nestled in the pillows again, ready for a nap. I was tired of talking. Damn, I was tired of breathing.

Though, I had to admit, seeing dragon eggs would be awesome, but right now I didn't have any energy left.

Shane sat down with me and like we had done before, I snuggled against him as my breathing slowed and I welcomed sleep. However, before I could really sleep, the door burst open again and wind blew over us.

"Kaz is asking for Raika," Killian said, materializing beside us.

"What? Why?" Shane asked.

"He didn't explain, but he said it was urgent."

I groaned. "Can't he come here?"

"He's in one of the courtyards and he seems to be preparing something," Killian said. "With the eggs."

That got my attention—the little I still had.

"I can carry you," Shane said, his tone soft, caring.

I didn't want that. I wanted to tell him I could walk, but I could barely move my arms. I didn't even know how I was still conscious with so much exhaustion falling over me.

I nodded.

Shane picked me up, and alongside Killian, carried me to the courtyard. There was a small crowd here—Minsi, Tyren, Rue, Drake, Thea, Almae, Lavinia, Elisa, Zadkiel, Lyra, Etyx, and in the center, Kaz with the eggs.

Shane set me down in front of them, still holding my arms to keep me steady, and I would have squealed in delight if I could have. The eggs—eight of them—were the size of volleyballs, but an oval shape, and in the most beautiful colors I had ever seen: swirls of teal, purple, pink, dark blue, and orange. The membrane was thin enough that we could see the shape of the tiny dragons inside.

Kaz stared at me. "Dragon eggs need their mother's power to survive."

"W-what?"

"The mother passes on her power to the eggs so the dragons inside grown to the size of a big watermelon and develop the way they should—and with magic."

"So ... without their mother, they will what? Die?"

Kaz nodded. "The eggs will stop growing and the dragons inside will wilt away, and they won't hatch."

"Wait. What happens when a mother dragon dies before the eggs can hatch?"

"It's rare for that to happen now," he said with a frown. "It's rare to have eggs at all, but when that happens, another female dragon can pass some of her power to the eggs. It's never the same, but at least they will grow, hatch, and the dragons will be born healthy."

Shane grunted. "What are you saying?"

"I'm saying that maybe, just maybe, you can pass your dragon magic to them."

I gasped. "All of it?"

Kaz frowned. "Usually, a mother dragon passes her powers, bit by bit, as the dragons grow. Think of it like donating blood. You produce more and after a while, you're ready to do it again. But in this case, better than not having any power at all, maybe they can take it all from you in one go."

"You said earlier that if there was a way of taking it all, it might kill me," I said."

"Right," Thea said. "The dragon magic was so attached to her. Will it just leave her?"

Kaz nodded. "True, but this is different. It won't be forceful. If this works as it should, the dragon magic will willingly leave you to go to the eggs."

"And this would save her?" Almae asked, her tone hopeful.

"Hopefully, yes," Kaz said. "But it might still be painful, and I can't guarantee anything. I've never seen or heard anything like this."

I was dying anyway, wasn't I? "Let's do it."

Kaz offered me his hand. I reached for him, but Shane grabbed my hand instead. He leaned into me. "Are you sure?"

I squeezed his hand. "It'll work," I said, believing it. It had to work. This was a big win-win. I didn't die and there would be eight new dragons in a world where they were supposed to be extinct. "Have faith."

He brought our joined hands to his lips and placed a soft kiss atop my hand, then he helped me go to Kaz. Kaz held my arm with a vice grip and guided me to the center of the eight eggs.

"Lie down," he said, helping me to the ground. I lay on the cold, rough stone ground, and he gently picked up each egg and placed them around me, touching my legs and arms and waist. They vibrated and were oddly warm to the touch. Kaz faced everyone standing in the courtyard. "I'm not sure what will happen, just remember this is delicate. Please, be quiet, or if you can't, leave before we start." No one moved a muscle. Kaz looked back at me. "Do you remember how you took Paimon's power?"

"Not really," I confessed. "I was a little out of it at the time."

"All right, then I'll guide you through the process." He knelt beside me and the eggs. "Close your eyes and take a deep breath. Think of the dragon magic inside of you and only that."

I did as instructed. I could see the magic inside me, swirling through my organs, running through my veins, inside every cell. It had become a part of me as if I had been born with it.

"For now, focus on it," Kaz continued. "Let it come to the surface, to your fingertips."

Again, I followed his directions.

Instantly, my skin heated up. I heard gasps coming from my friends and family.

"Kaz, she'll lose control again," Almae said, worried.

"No, she won't," he said, almost too harsh. "She can do this."

I inhaled deeply and trusted Kaz's words. I could do this. I had to do this. "Keep going," I whispered.

"Gently, slowly, send the dragon's magic to the eggs," he instructed. "The magic might sense the eggs and want to rush out. If that happens, don't let it. Send it bit by bit. You don't want to overwhelm them."

I let out a long breath and imagined myself opening a faucet, just a little, so only a few drops could fall at a time. The dragon's magic trickled from me to the eggs. Instantly, the eggs moved, shaking more than before.

"Focus," Kaz said. "Don't think about what they are doing. Just think about feeding the magic to them." I wished it was that easy. With the eggs agitated and the tension around the courtyard, it was a miracle I still had a handle on the magic. "Keep going," he continued. "Very slowly. It's working."

"How long will this take?" Shane whispered.

"A while," Kaz said, irritated. "Raika, focus."

Right. The magic, the eggs. I opened the faucet a tiny bit more and a few more drops of the dragon's magic went to the eggs. I could feel it, the magic gladly leaving me, eager to go to the dragons, as if I had been the worst host it ever had.

I didn't know how long had passed, but I stayed there, sprawled on the ground with the eggs for a long time as the dragon's power drifted away from me.

"You're doing well," Kaz said. He was crouched somewhere near my head. "The eggs are growing, shining brighter. It's working."

That was a relief.

After a while, I felt it. The last of the dragon's magic, the bit that was melded into me, mixed into my bones, my muscles, my blood. I coaxed it to the eggs, but it wouldn't budge.

Come on!

I wanted this magic gone. Not because it was killing me, but because it didn't belong to me. It was powerful, unstable. Besides, now that I knew I could save eight baby dragons with it, I wanted it gone more than ever!

I gritted my teeth, clenched my hands, curled my toes, and pulled the magic with all I had. The magic latched itself to me, tugging hard at my insides. Pain flared from every inch of my body, as if I was ripping my flesh wide open. I screamed.

"It's killing her!" Shane barked. I could hear him struggling against Kaz to get to me.

"Stop, Shane," I rasped. "I can do this." I tugged at the magic and screamed again, arching my back as a deep ripple of pain cut through me.

Something like a pop echoed inside of me. The last of the magic lashed out like a whip, making me cry once more.

Then it was gone.

I opened my eyes and stared at the blue sky above the courtyard. My chest heaved, my heart raced, my body was drenched in sweat, my limbs numb.

"Raika?" Shane knelt beside me.

I glanced from him to Kaz, who stared at the eggs with wide eyes. "Did it work?"

He nodded. "Look."

I propped myself on my elbows and looked at the eggs. They were bigger than before, brighter, and the babies inside were agitated. "Incredible."

Thea and Almae rushed to my side and hovered their hands over my body. The two of them shared an amused glance before smiling at me. "The dragon's magic is gone!" Thea declared.

I knew it was, I could feel it. Though I still had Paimon's darkfire within me. I didn't think I could do anything about that, but I didn't feel bad about it.

Shane held my hand. "So ... she's not dying anymore?"

Thea and Almae shook their heads.

Shane pulled me to his lap and hugged me tight.

Minsi and Tyren ran forward, but Kaz raised both hands. "Careful with the eggs!"

They stopped. With Shane's help, I stepped away from the eggs and went to them. The four of us hugged, and I pulled Rue into our embrace. She was part of the family. Our friends surrounded us, all patting our backs and congratulating us, while Kaz shouted for everyone to back away from the eggs.

That was the first and only time I saw Kaz shouting.

Shane kept a tight arm around my waist the entire time. I

looked into his eyes and saw the pure, unbound relief in them. I felt the exact same. I rose to my tiptoes, pressing my lips to his in a quick, soft peck.

I was tired, like I had fought a damn battle, which in a way, I had, but now, everything was okay. Paimon was defeated. There was no Conri or Nortrix to terrorize us. Our pack was together and I wasn't dying.

We would be okay.

FOUR MONTHS LATER
SHANE

I PUT THE ROSE IN THE HOLE, FILLED IT UP WITH SOIL, PATTED down to make sure it was secure, and stood up. I took off the garden gloves and threw them beside the other garden tools.

"It looks great," Raika said, coming up behind me.

"I think so too." I admired my work. I wasn't a good gardener, never would be, but I had wanted to plant this rose myself.

It had been the one Aurora had given Minsi when we thought Raika had died. I shook my head, glad that was over. All that we had been through ...

It was the past now.

I put my arm around Raika's shoulders and glanced at the house standing before us. It was my old house, but it wasn't. When Raika recovered and we came back to the Nightshade pack lands four months ago, we started rebuilding the town. And by that I meant the entire pack, Ivy, Killian, Lavinia, and two dozen vampires who had been tasked with helping us. We started with the several houses along main street so the wolves would have places to live. Next, we fixed the rest of the main street, the square, the library and the school, so the kids would have something to do while the rest of us worked all day long.

But as we rebuilt, we made several changes, and some not so little, to erase the bad things that had happened here. For example, the square was now a large green area with a few stone paths and lots of shrubs and thin trees. No more pavement or benches where items could be hidden underneath.

The school had also changed a lot, from the facade to the layout, and the colors and materials used inside. We wanted it to look nothing like before so the wolves and kids who entered the building never remembered what they went through while in the old school.

The alpha's house was the other one we changed a lot, mostly for Minsi. The layout was almost the same as before, it was still a farmhouse style, but we changed the colors, the decoration, and made sure her bedroom was different from her previous one. We also added a new floor where Raika's and my suite was—and it included a sitting area, a small office for when I needed to work from home, and a double balcony that opened to the front and the back gardens. Now the house also had a new resident: Rue. She had become our mother-slash-grandmother a long time before, and there was no reason to keep her away from us. Of course, we had asked her if she wanted to move in, and she had become so emotional, she couldn't answer for an entire minute.

Next on the list were the infirmary and the town hall. The rest of town waited while we made the main parts functional, but we wouldn't rebuild everything, not yet. There was no reason to rebuild houses that wouldn't be occupied, so for now, we cleared the area of the old, burned structures and debris, making room for more green.

This time, though, there would be no crystals and no barrier protecting the town. We would be open from all sides to friends and enemies, and for that, we would soon resume training and a rotation of patrols and other security measures —I had bought several cameras, sensors, and silent alarms to be placed along the land borders so we could keep an eye on anything suspicious.

Because we would also be at the weather's mercy, we were preparing for winter. I had bought several snow plows to clear Main Street fast and efficiently, and also installed central heat in all of the houses and buildings. I urged people to go clothes shopping and buy thick coats, beanies, gloves, scarfs, and snow boots. We would need them from now on ... and sooner rather than later. It was the end of November, and we already had heavy snow earlier this week. There was more snow coming in a few days. This was a challenge, but we were ready for it.

Raika rested her head on my shoulder. "Thank you."

"For?"

"Being a great alpha." She turned to me, her chin on my shoulder. "Being a great, hot alpha who loves me."

A growl came from my throat. "Don't start. We don't have time for that."

She bit on her lower lip. "Are you sure?"

Dear moon ... I turned to her, my arm going around her waist, and brought my lips to hers.

She parted her mouth for me, let me kiss her for only a brief moment, then pulled back with a teasing smile. "We're going to be late."

"Then let's be late." I leaned into her again.

With a laugh, Raika stepped back. "Shane, this is your first official gathering back here. We can't be late."

She was right, as usual, but damn, now all I could think of was tearing her clothes off, pressing her against the wall, and taking her right there and right then.

I shifted my weight, my pants suddenly tight.

I groaned. "Fine."

We walked through the house. I washed my hands in the kitchen's sink, made sure I hadn't gotten my clothes dirty while planting the rose, grabbed a heavy casserole, then hand-in-hand, Raika and I walked down Main Street toward the green.

I looked around, admiring the houses and how it was turning out. It had been only four months since we defeated Paimon and decided to come back, but we had already done so much, and it was all because of the great people we had working on this.

Even Eike, the Whitecrest alpha, had come a few times to visit and sent some of his wolves to help out.

"After all the previous alpha did to you, it's the least we can do," he said.

I wasn't in a position to deny any help, even from another pack. In fact, the first time he had come over and offered help, I had an idea. I called all the alphas for a meeting. This time, the alphas of the Wildtail and Warhide packs were finally in a truce—their packs had almost torn up each other, and they stopped before their entire war became nothing more than a river of blood.

So, I proposed a council of alphas and betas. We didn't need to like each other; we didn't need to agree on everything. However, we would respect each other and our packs, we would avoid conflict at any cost, and if threatened by an outside force, the packs would come together and fight as one.

To my surprise, all the alphas and betas agreed, and we had our first official meeting a week ago. It was tense, but besides the peace holding up and the news of how far my pack was in rebuilding our town, there was nothing to report.

I hoped it continued that way. Though, knowing the short temper of alphas and betas, it was a matter of time before some disagreement ensued. And then I would remind them of our deal. No fighting, just respect and talking until we found common ground and were able to come to a decision.

"I dare to say the town will be better than before," Raika said, sounding pleased.

I nodded. "I think so too."

We arrived at the green, where most of the pack had already gathered, waiting for the party to start.

Several picnic blankets were spread out on the right, where Rue and Vianna played with the kids. Minsi was there with them, seated beside Rue and quiet as usual. She missed Aurora, but we had promised we would visit them soon, and Drake and Thea promised they too would visit and bring Aurora often.

Long wooden tables and benches had been placed on the left side of the green and that was where most people were.

Tyren and Hugh had invited some of their friends from the Whitecrest pack. Dom stood with his mate, Anne, beside one of the tables, looking way too sappy. When we came back, he reached out to her, and even though it had been slow in the beginning, they had been together ever since.

Lucille was seated at another table with Celina and Jena. She was still upset she hadn't found her mate and was sure she would be the cool aunt with a half dozen cats.

I teased her that wolves didn't really have a good relationship with cats and she cursed me from here to the underworld.

Ivy waved as we approached and Raika disentangled herself from me and ran to her sister. After the battle against Paimon, Ivy had been released from her temporary hold, but put on probation. One evil-demon-like act and she would be put behind bars forever. But she had assured everyone she was done with all of that. She had done it because Paimon had threatened her, and feeling alone, she had felt like she needed to, so he wouldn't abandon her too.

For now, she was here and helping us with renovations, especially the library since that was important to Raika. She had ordered thousands of books to replace the ones lost during the fire, and Raika was over the moon.

However, she said she wouldn't stay long. "I want to travel the world," she told us one night when we were drinking wine in front of the fireplace, after Minsi went to bed. "And then, I don't know. I might buy a small island, build a beautiful beach mansion, and live the rest of my days like a hermit."

"As long as you visit often," Raika said.

Ivy winked at her. "Of course. You can't get rid of me that easily."

For Raika's sake, I hoped Ivy really visited a lot. The two of them had developed a special bond, but I could see in Ivy, when she thought no one was looking, how her past weighed on her. If left alone, she might fall into a deep depression.

Which reminded me of Ariella. We hadn't heard from her in the past four months, and I worried about her mental health. She had first lost her wings, then her powers. It might be too hard for her to live right now. I wished she hadn't left, but other than keeping an eye out for her, there wasn't much I could do.

As for Kaz, he had taken the eight dragon eggs to wherever it was he and the other dragon shifters and dragons hid. Despite his usually closed off stance, he seemed pretty pleased about having new dragons.

It was a good thing Lyra had gone to the mountain to help the goblins. She had been the one who insisted on scouring every inch of the mountain to find the demons hiding there and kill them so they would stop terrorizing and killing the goblins. If she hadn't done that, they would never have found the eggs. And Etyx had come back with her to thank me, Drake and the vampires personally, in Sloz's name.

"We had our doubts, but yer help was invaluable," he said. "Ye can always count on us."

I approached the table with all of the food. Instead of a barbecue, we had decided on a potluck. I placed the casserole beside the other plates, my mouth watering at the sight of so many good things: corn on the cob, fried chicken wings, pizza bites, mini pot pies, mini quiche, cheese bites, and desserts.

Beside the tables, coolers held the drinks and I grabbed a cold beer.

Hamill appeared by my side and slapped my shoulder before I could take a sip. "Ready for your speech?"

I hated speeches, but today was a special day. "We'll find out."

My phone buzzed and I glanced at the screen. A text from Evelyn popped up.

How's the party?

I shook my head. I would answer her later. I was still upset she and Ash hadn't come. They were still in Mexico, following another trail of dragon bones—but Evelyn maintained contact with Kaz, and if she found any, she handed them over to him. However, right now they were in Cozumel on a well-deserved vacation.

Killian and Lavinia put down a plate with cinnamon pastries on the table.

I frowned. "You two are eating?"

Killian shrugged. "It's not like we can't."

"And these are way too good to pass up," Lavinia said with a smile. Before all of this, before becoming a full witch and then a vampire, Lavinia worked at a coffeeshop and had an older friend, and witch, who had been a baker, and she had taught Lavinia all she knew.

I glanced at Killian. He was still an honorary member of my pack's council, and he would be for as long as he wanted, but a couple of weeks ago, he did mention "retiring" from the position once the town was rebuilt and we had everything under control.

"I think I would like to live at DuMoir Castle with Lavinia permanently," he said. "But you're not getting rid of us. We'll visit often."

I frowned, remembering that conversation. It seemed everyone wanted to follow their own calls. While it was understandable, it made me sad. Our pack, our family, had become so vast and strong with our friends and allies, it was hard to see them all leaving, even if they promised to visit often.

"Any news from Cain and Norah?" I asked. I always did.

Killian shook his head. "Drake has plenty of vampires around the world, searching for a portal key. Without one, there's no way to bring them back."

"We don't even know if there is another one," Lavinia said, her voice low. "At least they have each other."

"Maybe now they will stop playing cat and mouse and finally give in to their mating bond," Killian said. "By the time we find a way to rescue them, they will be sick of each other."

I glanced at Raika a few feet from us as she laughed about something Ivy said. My heart squeezed, the always-there tug pushing me to her. I couldn't imagine ever getting sick of her.

"I think everyone is here," Hamill announced. "It's time for your speech."

I groaned as I stepped on one of the benches so everyone could see me.

"Good evening," I said to my family, friends, and pack members as they all walked closer and faced me. "I'll be brief, I promise."

Chuckles echoed through them.

I cleared my throat. "Our pack has been through a lot. So many wrong turns, hardships, and trials, I couldn't count on my fingers. But we endured. We stayed strong and true to our hearts, and we made it. We emerged on the other side even stronger and braver, and more importantly, united. After what we've been through, we know we can take on anything and anyone, and we'll survive." I paused. "Though I hope those days are far behind us." Lots of heads nodded. "Today marks a new beginning for the Nightshade pack. Every year, we'll celebrate this day as the 'New Day.' We'll remember and honor our fallen, and we'll renew our bond and unity." I raised my beer high. "To a new day!"

"To a new day!" everyone repeated after me.

"It's time to celebrate," I said.

Cheers followed. Music played from the small speaker placed on the table and the party seemed to finally start as people started dancing beside the tables. The sun lowered behind the trees and the sky became a beautiful, stained painting of dark orange, purple, and dark blue.

An arm hooked mine and tugged me backward.

With a smile, I turned and let Raika guide me to the improvised dance floor. Swaying side to side, she wrapped her arms around my shoulders. I followed her rhythm and I splayed my hands on her back, securing her closer to me.

After getting rid of the dragon's magic, Raika remained in the infirmary at DuMoir Castle for one more day. Thea and Almae wanted to be sure she was one hundred percent well before releasing her. And, despite having Paimon's darkfire within her, Raika was as healthy as anyone could be. It was as if she had never had a power that was killing her.

My chest constricted. To think I had almost lost her three times, I couldn't bear. But Raika was strong, the strongest of all of us. While I fell into my own despair believing I was alone, she had been the one strong piece that held this pack together for an entire year. We owed it all to her. I owed it all to her—my sanity, my peace, my happiness.

"Great speech," she said. "If I wasn't in love with you, I would have fallen for you right then."

I chuckled. "Oh, so speeches turn you on."

She raised her eyebrows. "I like when you talk while we …" Her cheeks gained a pink tint. By the moon, this woman was too beautiful for her own good.

I leaned into her and whispered in her ear, "How about we go for a run and visit an old place of ours?"

Her breath hitched. She knew I was talking about the fissure where the bond first snapped. We had made love once outside the fissure, never inside. The walls were too rough, but if I brought a blanket to wrap around us …

My pants tightened again.

"The first one there gets to call the shots," she whispered back, then ran from me. I stared at her, stunned and amused as she darted from the party, giggling.

Some heads turned, but by now the entire pack knew us—we couldn't keep our hands off each other.

I smiled and set off after her.

Wherever she went, I followed.

Forever.

I HOPE YOU ENJOYED RAIKA+SHANE'S STORY! IF YOU HAVEN'T read the other books in the Rite World universe, then check them all out on this page on my website—including recommended reading order and links!

THANK YOU

Thank you for reading *The Night Rising*!

Reviews are very important for authors. If you liked my book, please consider leaving a review on your favorite online retailer and/or on Goodreads and/or Bookbub, please!

Did you like this book? You can check out other books of mine:

The Darkest Vampire (Rite World: Vampire Wars book 1): a witch releases a dark vampire from a curse, and becomes inadvertently bonded to him.

The Midnight Test (Rite World: Lightgrove Witches book 1): a clueless witch is invited to join a powerful coven—but only if she aces a difficult test.

The Demon Kiss (Rite World: Blackthorn Hunters Academy book 1): a fast-paced story about a young woman who finds out she's a demon hunter, and the half-demon intent on protecting her against all evil.

The Vampire Heir (Rite World 1: Rite of the Vampire): a

dark and mysterious paranormal romance about a vampire and a young woman with a secret.

The Warlock Lord (Rite World 4: Rite of the Warlock): a thrilling and kick-ass paranormal romance about a werewolf and warlock.

The Wolf Forsaken (Rite World 7: Rite of the Wolf): a heat-wrenching tale about a lost wolf shifter and a fae princess on the run.

Heart Seeker (The Fire Heart Chronicles book 1): an urban fantasy series about a young woman who finds herself at the center of a mysterious supernatural world.

Destiny Gift (The Everlast Series book 1): a post-apocalyptic urban fantasy series about a young woman with a special power that can save the world.

Don't forget to sign up for my Newsletter to find out about new releases, cover reveals, giveaways, and more!

If you want to see exclusive teasers, help me decide on covers, read excerpts, talk about books, etc, join my reader group on Facebook: Juliana's Club!

ABOUT THE AUTHOR

While USA Today Bestselling Author Juliana Haygert dreams of being Wonder Woman, Buffy, or a blood elf shadow priest, she settles for the less exciting—but equally gratifying—life as a wife, a mother, and an author. She resides in North Carolina and spends her days writing about kick-ass heroines and the heroes who drive them crazy.

Subscribe to her mailing list to receive emails of announcement, events, and other fun stuff related to her writing and her books: www.bit.ly/JuHNL

For more information:
www.julianahaygert.com

facebook.com/julianahaygert

twitter.com/julianahaygert

instagram.com/juliana.haygert

goodreads.com/juliana_haygert

pinterest.com/julianahaygert

bookbub.com/authors/juliana-haygert

youtube.com/julianahaygert

tiktok.com/@julianahaygert

ALSO BY JULIANA HAYGERT

To find links and more info, go to:
www.julianahaygert.com/books/

Shorts
Into the Darkest Fire

Standalones
Daughter of Darkness

Rite World: Night Wolves
The Night Calling (Book 1)
The Night Burning (Book 2)
The Night Hunting (Book 3)
The Night Rising (Book 4)

Rite World: Vampire Wars
The Darkest Vampire (Book 1)
The Darkest Witch (Book 2)
The Darkest Magic (Book 3)

Rite World: Lightgrove Witches
The Midnight Test (Book 1)
The Midnight Spell (Book 2)
The Midnight Flame (Book 3)

Rite World: Blackthorn Hunters Academy
The Demon Kiss (Book 1)
The Hunter Secret (Book 2)
The Soul Bond (Book 3)
The Shadow Trials (Book 4)
The Infernal Curse (Book 5)

<u>*Rite World*</u>
The Vampire Heir (Book 1)
The Witch Queen (Book 2)
The Immortal Vow (Book 3)
The Warlock Lord (Book 4)
The Wolf Consort (Book 5)
The Crystal Rose (Book 6)
The Wolf Forsaken (Book 7)
The Fae Bound (Book 8)
The Blood Pact (Book 9)

<u>*The Wyth Courts*</u>
Winter King (Book 1)
Spring Warrior (Book 2)
Summer Prince (Book 3)
Autumn Rebel (Book 4)

<u>*The Fire Heart Chronicles*</u>
Heart Seeker (Book 1)
Flame Caster (Book 2)
Earth Shaker (Book 2.5)
Sorrow Bringer (Book 3)
Soul Wanderer (Book 4)
Fate Summoner (Book 5)
War Maiden (Book 6)

<u>*The Everlast Series*</u>
Destiny Gift (Book 1)
Soul Oath (Book 2)
Cup of Life (Book 3)
Everlasting Circle (Book 4)

<u>*Willow Harbor Series*</u>
Hunter's Revenge (Book 3)
Siren's Song (Book 5)

Breaking Series
Breaking Free (Book 1)
Breaking Away (Book 2)
Breaking Through (Book 3)
Breaking Down (Book 4)